Our Little Crusader Cousin of Long Ago

This edition published 2026
by Living Book Press
Copyright © Living Book Press, 2026

ISBN: 978-1-76183-126-3 (hardcover)
         978-1-76183-124-9 (softcover)

First published in 1921.

A catalogue record for this book is available from the National Library of Australia

Our little Crusader Cousin of Long Ago

by

EVALEEN STEIN

Hugh
Raymond

Contents

Preface

I wonder if you boys and girls know what the crusades were? Perhaps not; so in as few pages as I can I will try to give you a little idea of them, though when you grow older you will find there are no end of interesting things to learn about them.

In the first place we must go back a long way, to the year 1000, when, for some reason or other, people in Europe got it into their heads that because it was a thousand years from the birth of Christ the world would surely come to an end. They were so certain of it that they thought a great deal about their sins and what would become of them in the next world. Many of them even sold all they had and spent their time making pilgrimages from one holy place to another; for they believed that to go on foot and pray at these shrines would benefit them greatly in the life to come. Some went to shrines of saints near their homes, some to the city of Rome and elsewhere; but of course the most sacred place of all to visit was Jerusalem, where is the tomb of our Saviour. To pray at this, the Holy Sepulchre, as it was most often called, these pilgrims longed to do more than anything else. Those who had done so were called "palmers" because they always wore in their hats a bit of palm which they brought from the Holy Land, and they no doubt were not a little proud that they had made the long and perilous journey in safety. For in those days to go to Jerusalem was indeed a hard and danger-ous undertaking, requiring many months, sometimes years.

Some went by land, passing through many countries and enduring great hardships; while others, going to some port on the Mediterranean sea,—you know Palestine is on the eastern coast of this,—sailed in boats, usually small and crowded and little able to withstand storm and shipwreck. And worst of all, when at last the weary pilgrim reached the holy city he was liable to be beaten or robbed or perhaps killed by the Turks, or Saracens, as most people called them, who ruled over Palestine. The Saracens did not believe in our Christian religion, but in their own prophet Mohammed; so they looked with contempt on the pilgrims and treated them very cruelly.

Now of course you know the world did not come to an end in the year 1000. But the European people were still frightened, and decided that they must have made a mistake and that it would end a thousand years from the crucifixion of our Lord instead of from his birth. So for thirty-two years more they made pilgrimages harder than ever. At the end of that time they found that most of them were still alive and the world behaving about as usual and with no signs of the Day of Judgment; perhaps it was to show their relief and thankfulness to God because of this, or perhaps simply because so many had gotten in the habit of it, but at any rate pilgrims still thronged to Jerusalem and the Saracens treated them worse and worse all the time.

Of course the pilgrims brought back many stories of cruelty and of how the infidels (that means people who do not believe in our religion, and was another name for the Saracens) desecrated even the tomb of our Saviour; and these stories made their friends at home more and more angry and indignant. At last things came

to a climax when a French monk, named Peter the Hermit, went to Jerusalem and was so badly treated that on his way home he stopped at Rome and told Pope Urban about things there. Peter spoke so well that the Pope wept over the story, and going to France with Peter, he called together a large company, in which were many of the greatest princes and noblest knights of the land.

The Pope told them the things he had heard, and then begged them to stop fighting and quarreling among themselves, as many of them had been doing, and to go to the Holy Land and take the Holy Sepulchre away from the Saracens; indeed, to conquer Jerusalem and all Palestine so that Christians might go there and worship in peace.

Before the Pope was through speaking, everybody had become so excited that suddenly as with one voice the multitude shouted, "God wills it!" "God wills it!" and pressing forward, vowed that they would go and fight for the Holy Land and the tomb of Christ. At this Pope Urban said, "Let this then be your war-cry, 'God wills it!'" And in token that they were going to fight and shed their blood for Christ, each man received a cross of red cloth, which was fastened upon his sleeve; and having once taken this cross, it was considered cowardly and disgraceful to turn back from the undertaking.

But they did not turn back. The princes and knights set

to work to raise great armies, and knights and soldiers from other countries joined them. It all took a long while, but at last they were ready, and in the year 1096 they set off for Palestine; and because of the red cross every man wore, the expedition was called a "crusade" and the soldiers "crusaders."

Long and hard was the journey; thousands died on the way from sickness and hardships and fighting enemies in countries through which they passed. But at last the crusaders reached Palestine, which they finally conquered after many months of gallant fighting. Indeed, the fame of the heroes of that first crusade is still handed down in poetry and stories. Of course, having conquered the country, they could not all go away and leave it at the mercy of the Saracens, who would all the while be trying to get it back again. So many of the leaders sent for their wives and children and planned to stay there, building castles and living much as they did at

spring. As soon as April came Philip sailed for the Holy Land; but as some of the English supply ships had not yet come, Richard had to wait a few weeks longer;—and this brings us to the beginning of our story, which starts in June, 1191.

There were other crusades after the one our story is about, seven in all, and many are the gallant heroes of these whose names have been handed down to us; but for his marvelous daring and unsurpassed bravery, his kingly spirit and his romantic life none has so captured the world's fancy as has King Richard of the Lion Heart, who is even now on his way sailing into our little story.

CHAPTER I

Richard the Lion Heart Lands in Palestine

Far Away, on the coast of Palestine, beyond the ancient city of Acre the slopes of Mount Carmel gleamed bright green in the June sunlight: pink and white oleanders, blue myrtle bloom, golden daises and countless other of the gay flowers that flourish in that warm country dotted the green, and here and there rose tall, feathery palm trees crowned with clusters of ripening dates. But though the mountain was bright with color, the sandy plain beside the city walls was gray with tattered tents of war from which floated banners and pennons once brilliant and glowing but now faded in the burning sun of the East; for the crusading army besieging Acre had been camped there for two years.

To be sure, along the shore there showed now beside this older camp the fresher tents of the French host and the silken one of King Philip with its standard sown with golden lilies. But though these new crusaders from France had been welcomed with such joy nearly two months before, and though they had helped batter and pound the walls of Acre almost every day since then, still the great stone towers were stout and strong, the city still untaken. And more than this, Saracen soliders and their allies, a mixed horde of Turks, Moors, Arabs and Egyptians (though I call them all, as did many of the crusaders, simply "Saracens"), were all the while gathering to help the people of Acre, and had begun to besiege the besiegers themselves, around their camp and be constantly on the watch for attacks from behind while they were trying in vain to storm the city.

(Before I go any farther, I wonder, have you children read the Preface of this story? If not you had best hurry up and do so or you will not understand things nearly so well. It is not very long, and though I am going right on with the story, if you are quick about it you can soon catch up.)

It is no wonder then that all the Christian army, especially those who had been there two whole years, were hoping and praying for the fleet of Richard to sail in sight, for they felt sure that with the coming of the lion-hearted king the city must surely be captured. For weeks they had looked anxiously to the west across the waters of the Mediterranean, but it was not till the June morning when our story begins that a soldier who had climbed up the slopes white away off on the horizon, and flashing in front of it a gleam of red. Then more and more white rose over the sea, and with a glad cry, "King Richard is coming!" he flew down to the camp, and in a moment, as the word sped from mouth to mouth, the shore was lined with an eager throng, all breathlessly watching as nearer and nearer drew the English fleet.

On and on they came, oars flashing, sails swelling, ships and ships of every kind, almost two hundred of them. Soon rose the sound of trumpets from the foremost one, sweeping far ahead of all, flying scarlet sails and red as a poppy from stem to stern. "Look! Look!" "King Richard's ship, the *Trenchmer!*" shouted the French soliders; for while in Sicily they had seen the royal vessel, whose name means "seacutter."

And very gay and splendid it looked, its scarlet sides glittering in the sun, its deck fluttering with the bright pennons of the noble knights who crowded to its rail. At either end of the ship was a high platform with castle-like turrets, and on this were the trumpeters blowing as hard as ever they could. But it was on the prow of the vessel that caught the attention of all. There flew the royal standard of England with its three lions, and close beside it stood a tall, powerfully built and strikingly handsome man who bore himself with the most noble dignity. Over his hauberk of chain mail hung a purple mantle fastened with a richly jeweled clasp; his head was uncovered, and his tawny yellow hair, curling about his neck, shone in the light. As he stood motionless, with folded arms, his clear blue eyes fixed on the land seemed not to see the excited throng waiting there, but to be looking into some great dream of his own; and then, just as the ship was getting ready to anchor, with a sudden quick gesture flinging his mantle back and moving to the rail, he plunged into the sea, and wading breast-high to the shore, reverently knelt and touched his lips to the sacred soil. Thus it was that King Richard of the Lion Heart landed, first of all the fleet.

For a few moments the waiting crowd had stood speechless, watching the king, but the instant he rose to his feet such a shout of joy went up that even the Saracens in the besieged city began to mount the walls and peer over the battlements; and their hosts of allies camped along the shore ventured nearer to glimpse this wonderful new hero who had come to fight them and whose fame had already spread across the sea.

As for the crusaders, they were simply wild with joy, and while King Philip was welcoming Richard they hurriedly formed processions, marching up and down, beating drums, blowing trumpets, and fairly shouting themselves hoarse.

Meantime the knights and their followers were flocking off the *Trenchmer*, and among them came a boy in the dress of a page, a tunic of Lincoln green, long black hose, a short scarlet cape and small velvet cap with a pheasant's feather; on one sleeve of his tunic was embroidered a red cross, on the other three leopards. His fair hair and dark eyes spoke his mixed Saxon and Norman blood; and as he eagerly scanned the people on shore suddenly his face lighted as a dark-haired boy of about his own age sprang toward him, and with a glad "Hugh!" and "Raymond!" they tumbled into each other's arms. The two lads, both pages, Hugh, as the leopards on his sleeve shoed, serving King Richard, and Raymond attending Count William de Pratelles of France, had met during the winter the armies had spent in Sicily and had become warm friends;

though of course they had been separated when King Philip sailed first for Palestine.

As Hugh now gazed wonderingly around, "Why!" he said, "it looks as if people were here from every country in the world!"

"Yes," answered Raymond, "I believe they are. Ever since we've been here; that group of newer tents yonder are Austrians who got here in a short time ago with their Duke Leopold, and the older crusaders say that for two or three years little parties of soldiers have been landing from nearly everywhere. Did you ever in your life see so many different banners and so many queer-looking people and queer clothes?"

"No indeed!" said Hugh, continuing to gaze around. And Raymond was certainly right; the people were of many races, and their clothes of innumerable kinds, yet none in the least like we are used to seeing soldiers wear. What kind were they, then? Well, the Saracens had loose robes girdled in various ways, and turbans of many folds of silk or linen wrapped around their heads to protect them from the hot sun. The crusader's dress was usually some kind of long tunic of linen or wool, and cross-gartered hose; and when the knights put on their armor they wore over it another loose, sleeveless tunic, called a surcoat, often richly embroidered, and meant, like the turbans of their enemies, to protect them from the heat. For most of them had come from cooler countries and had found that the sun of Palestine could make their metal armor as hot as an oven.

But while Hugh was still staring, "Look!" cried Raymond, "the other biggest ships have anchored, and there are ladies on one! See! King Philip is lifting one of them ashore in his arms! Who is she? I didn't see her in Sicily."

"That is the Princess Berengaria of Navarre," answered Hugh. "No, I mean Queen Barengaria. King Richard married her in Cyprus only a week ago. I will tell you about it when we get time to talk. Isn't she a beauty? And that other handsome lady is Queen Joan, King Richard's sister,—she used to be queen of Sicily. They have a lot of noble ladies with them and they are all going along with the army."

"Well," said Raymond, "there are a good many ladies in camp now, wives of the different knights who live here, so I guess they won't be lonesome. But look at the big chests they are taking off the third ship! I suppose that is King Richard's treasure ship. King Philip had one; it's over there in the harbor now."

"Yes," said Hugh, "and I don't wonder they have to have big chests of gold. It must take an enormous amount of money to pay so many soldiers and buy things for them to eat."

"I should think so!" echoed Raymond. "You know all our ships carried a year's supply of stuff to eat, but when we came, things were getting so scarce with the army that had been here so long that we had to let them have some of our food. The crusaders, though, haven't suffered anything like the folks shut up in the city there. They say they are nearly starved, for of course the armies camped here won't let anything get inside the gates. They think the Saracens outside do manage to sneak in a few things for the Acre people, but it can't be much, and they must be mighty hungry."

"Well," said Hugh, "King Richard started with a year's supply, too, and he has brought besides a lot of grain and fruit and wine and I don't know what all from Cyprus, so I guess there will be enough to last our armies for a while.

Meantime the new-comers were being shown the place allotted to them for their camp and the soldiers were beginning to pitch the tents; so the two pages scampered off to see if they were needed for any service.

All day long the crusaders swarmed about, unloading ships and arranging the new camp, and though much was still to be done, by nightfall the quarters were ready for the more important people. The gay silken pavilions for the two queens and their ladies were pitched at a safe distance from any possible fighting and were piled with cushions spread with rich coverings; and before the handsome tent of King Richard in the midst of the camp was planted the English standard and his own banner with its three leopards.

When it grew dark great bonfires were lighted, and all the soldiers feasted and shouted and sang and spent nearly the whole night rejoicing. Hugh and Raymond were so excited they could hardly sleep at all when, near dawn, they threw themselves on their beds, each in a tent adjoining that of his master. The two kings however were not with the rejoicing throng. In Richard's tent for hours they talked over the crusade and tried to plan what would be their next move against Acre; and when they parted, both looked tired and worn. For Philip was barely recovered from the fever which had attacked him in Palestine and which had carried off so many of the crusaders who were unused to the climate; and Richard, who had been sailing down the coast for several days, was beginning also to feel the seeds of this same sickness.

CHAPTER II

Hugh Tells of the Voyage

The next morning Hugh did a number of errands for King Richard, and then the latter, who was fond of the lad, told him he might run along and look around a bit with his friend Raymond. Hugh at once hurried over toward the French camp, and though Raymond had told him in what direction to look for Count William's tent, he was quite uncertain of finding it among so many thousands. But luckily he had not gone far when he spied Raymond holding the bridle of a war-horse his master was mounting. He was going with a company of French knights to see if they could find some Saracens thought to be hiding in the hills and trying to bring food to the besieged city.

As soon as Count William rode off the two pages ran down to the shore to watch the rest of the ships being unloaded. These were of many kinds and sizes; as no one then had dreamed of steamboats, and all had sails, and long rows of oars, too. The smaller ones were called galleys and the larger "busses" and "dromonds;" these last usually had one deck and a few cabins below, and carried about two hundred men, including fifty knights and their horses, and provisions for a year. At each end was built up a platform where trumpeters could sit, or, more important when the ship was in a fight, where archers could be stationed: for gunpowder was not yet invented. Also, at the top of the mast was a little cage-like place to which archers could climb by means of a rope ladder. These ships were thought very large and fine in those days, though to us they would look very small and queer.

As the two boys watched, "Look!" said Raymond, "that must be King Richard's horse they are taking off the *Trench-mer*. See how careful they are with him and how proudly he steps along. But, Hugh," he added, as he eyed the horse more critically, "that's not the one he had in Sicily; that was a black one from Spain, I remember."

"Yes," said Hugh, "it was, but he likes this one better; he got him in the island of Cyprus on the way here, and his name is Favelle. Isn't he handsome? And they say the jewels on his harness and trappings are worth a fortune, and besides these the stirrups and all the trimmings of the saddle are pure gold and on his crupper are two little golden lions pawing each other! And there come more of the knights' horses, all with their armor!" For war-horses, then were protected by armor, the same as their masters.

"And they will find it mighty hot and uncomfortable in this country!" said Raymond. "I've seen the horses and knights, too, just panting after they have been fighting a while. I guess the Saracens know better how to do in a climate like this. They ride the fastest kind of Arabian horses and carry just light shields, and they seem to depend more on shooting their arrows and then getting out of the way quickly. Of course in hand-to-hand fighting our crusaders can smash harder with their battle-axes and things."

"I see the armies here have a good many fighting machines," said Hugh, "but I believe King Richard has brought some better ones. There are some of them now coming off yonder galleys," and he pointed to the hughe wooden structures being set up on the beach; some were for pounding through city walls, and were called "battering-rams" because of the ram's head of copper fastened on the end of the great beam of wood which did the pounding and which was hung by ropes to a strong framework. There were other ropes fastened to the beam and it sometimes took hundreds of men to pull it back and forth. Other of the machines were called catapults, petraries and mangonels and were made to shoot arrows or hurl stones a great distance.

As the boys eyed these machines, "You know," went on Hugh, "they are the ones King Richard had built in Sicily last winter because he thought wood was scarce over here. He even brought stones for the catapults. Do you see that pile there on the beach?" "Yes," answered Raymond, "it was a good thing he got them ready in Sicily. Wood and stones are scarce here. And just a few days ago our French army was attacking the city walls and the Saracens poured down some Greek fire and burned up two of King Philip's biggest machines. That Greek fire is horrible! A lot of soldiers have been burned to death by its getting under their armor, and water won't put it out. I never say anything like it before."

"I saw some of it on the way here, when King Richard fought the Saracen ship," said Hugh.

"What all did King Richard do on the way?" asked Raymond. "We didn't stop anywhere or have any adventures!" he added regretfully.

"Well," said Hugh, "things generally are moving when King Richard is around. Didn't we have a fine exciting winter in Sicily when he was fighting King Tancred there?"

"Yes, indeed!" answered Raymond, his eyes sparkling. "I never did know, though, what the quarrel was about; you know King Philip kept out of it."

"There was reason enough to fight," said Hugh. "It seems the husband of Queen Joan, King Richard's sister, used to be king of Sicily, and when he died a while ago Tancred got himself made king and shut up Queen Joan and took away all her money. He earned the good beating he got!"

"Did they make up afterward?" asked Raymond. "You know about that time we sailed for here with King Philip."

"Yes," said Hugh, "they gave each other presents, and then King Richard invited everybody to a big feast in honor of his betrothal to Princess Berengaria. His mother, Queen Eleanor, had brought her from Navarre, somewhere near Spain, where her father is king. King Richard couldn't go after her himself, because he had started on the crusade, but he wanted to get married and take her along."

"But I thought you said yesterday they were married in Cyprus," said Raymond, looking rather bewildered.

"So they were," answered Hugh, "for when the princess got to Sicily,—it was just after you left,—it was Lent, you know, and it's against the church rules to have grand weddings then. So they thought, as Lent would soon be over, they would stop at Rhodes, one of the islands on the way, and get married there. King Richard had that handsome ship over there fitted up for the ladies, for Queen Joan decided to come, too, and he sent along some of our best knights to guard them. You just ought to have seen us start away from Sicily. I believe everybody there was out to see us off! It was a fine bright day, and we had flags flying and music playing and everything lively. When it got dark they lighted the big red lantern on the mast of the *Trenchmer*—see it over there?—so the others could follow our ship. But in a little while there was a terrible storm came up."

"Were you scared?" asked Raymond.

"Yes," admitted Hugh, after a moment's hesitation, "I was. The storm lasted two days and I thought surely we should all upset and be drowned! Several of the ships were wrecked and blown to pieces, a lot of them ran up on little islands, and the third day we managed to put into the harbor at Rhodes. The *Trenchmer* was pretty badly battered up, but when King Richard looked around and saw the ladies' ship wasn't there he wouldn't stay, but gave orders to sail right on for Cyprus, which was the next big island. He thought maybe he would find the princess there. The next day we sighted Cyprus, and there was the ladies' ship standing off outside the harbor of a town."

"Why were they *outside* the harbor?" asked Raymond.

"That was what King Richard wanted to know," replied Hugh. "So he sent two sailors and one of our knights in the *Trenchmer's* little life-boat to see what was the matter: and the captain of the ladies' ship told them that two others of our galleys had been wrecked on the coast and when the men tried to swim ashore the Cyprus people beat them off so they could get all the valuable things that floated. They acted so mean that the captain didn't dare land with the ladies. When our folks came back and told King Richard that, he was simply furious!"

"What did he do?" inquired Raymond, who was listening with interest.

"Do?" eachoed Hugh, "why, the wind wasn't toward the harbor so we could sail in, but he ordered the rowers to get the *Trenchmer* there as fast as they could. Then we all hurried ashore and King Richard sent for the king of Cyprus, whose name was Isaac. When Isaac showed fight and wouldn't apologize for the outrageous way his people acted about the wreck, King Richard just grabbed his big battle-ax—you know how enormous it is—and waving it in the air, he rushed toward the town to attack it. All our knights went after him, and a good many from some other ships that had come up, and before long King Richard had taken the town.

And right away he signalled for the ladies' ship to come on, and he took Princess Berengaria and Queen Joan and their maids of honor and put them in Isaac's best palace. Then he took another fine palace for himself, and all the knights had very grand houses to stay in."

"What became of Isaac?" put in Raymond. "At first he promised everything King Richard wanted," replied Hugh, "but when King Richard found he was all the while plotting behind his back, he made him prisoner. Isaac cried and made such a fuss about being chained up that King Richard said his chains should be silver because he had been a king. He looked pretty scornful, though, when he said it, and put a good strong guard over him, so I guess Isaac will never get Cyprus back again."

"How long did you stay there?" asked Raymond.

"A whole month," answered Hugh, "and then came the wedding. It was the grandest affair! King Richard looked magnificent; he had on a bright rose-colored satin tunic and a mantle of striped silver tissue all embroidered with jewels, and his belt and sword were sparkling with more jewels, and on his head was a kind of cap of red velvet brocaded with gold lions, and he carried a gold scepter in his hand. The Princess Berengaria looked like a fairy beside him,—you saw how little she is. She wore a wonderful white dress, with lots of gold and diamonds," he added vaguely, for he could remember Richard's costume better than his bride's. "And then," he went on. "I helped carry in the dishes at the feast afterward, and I was worn out when it was over. I never saw so many fine things to eat in all my life, and everything was served on gold and silver platters, for we used all Isaac's best things and he was very rich. Right away after the feast we loaded up the ships again and started for here."

"When was it you fought the Saracen ship?" was Raymond's next question.

"Why that was two days after we left Cyprus," replied Hugh. "It was the biggest ship I ever saw. King Richard thought it must have held nearly fifteen hundred men!"

"Whew!" exclaimed Raymond, with round eyes. "I didn't know ships *could* be so big!"

"Neither did I," said Hugh, "but it was. It seems it was carrying food and money for Acre here; I suppose they thought they could sneak it into the city some way. The ship was so big that King Richard knew the *Trenchmer* couldn't fight it alone, so he ordered six more of our fleet to line up in a row and they all started to ram the Saracen one. It was then the Saracens began throwing Greek fire on ours. They threw vases full of it,—it's a kind of liquid, you know,—and when the vases smashed, it caught fire in the air, and it got on some of the sailors and burned them to death!"

"Did the rams make a hole in the ship?" asked Raymond.

"Yes," said Hugh, "and when the Saracens saw that, they began to chop more holes as fast as they could, for they wanted the ship to sink before our men could climb on it. I guess they thought they would rather drown than fall into the hands of our crusaders, and then, too, they didn't want us to get all the food and treasure they had on board. But King Richard and the rest hurried and climbed on it and got most of the things off and put on our ships. The Saracens fought like everything, but unless they could swim somewhere I don't think many were alive when our fighters got through with them. Some of our men were killed but most got back all right to our ships, and then we sailed on for Palestine. When King Richard first caught sight of the coast he said two words I couldn't understand,—one of the knights said they were Latin and meant 'Holy Land'—and then he never took his eyes off it, but just stood watching it in a kind of dream till we landed."

"Well," said Raymond, drawing a long breath, "of course our trip here was all very strange and new to me but it was nothing like so exciting as yours!"

But by this time the boys knew they had better be going back to their masters, so they parted for the day.

CHAPTER III

In the Camp Before Acre

It was more than a week after the landing of the English fleet and their new camp was in fairly good order, but none of the leaders of the crusade were in a particularly good humor and many of the foot-soldiers were growing every day more impatient because no progress had been made toward the taking of Acre. Everybody had hoped for so much with the coming of King Richard, but for days he had been stretched on his bed tossing and burning with the terrible fever that had attacked so many of the crusaders, and which of course was the reason he was not in a good humor. King Phillip was irritable and cross because he himself was still not entirely over the same kind of fever, though he had not been nearly so sick as Richard; and then he did not like the delay, and moreover he and Richard were not really very good friends anyway, and only tried to keep at peace with one another on account of the crusade. Then there was the Austrian Duke Leopold, who was out of sorts because he was a stupid man with a high opinion of himself and he thought King Richard had snubbed him, which likely he had as he had a great contempt for Duke Leopold.

As for the people of Acre, no doubt they were all the while

getting hungrier and crosser; and the Sultan Saladin with his army of Saracens camped on the hills behind Acre and his allies beyond the moat of the crusaders were becoming tired with their constant watching.

But if affairs were not going in a way to please the grown folks on either side, our two boys found no end of things to interest them. Everything was so strange and different from their own homes, and until starting on the crusade neither had ever traveled anywhere. And this reminds me that I have not yet told you where their homes were nor how it happened that, though one came from England and the other from France, they had no trouble in talking to each other. That was because many of the English nobles, of who Hugh's father was one, and especially King Richard himself, though born in England, seemed really to belong much more to France and spoke French almost altogether. And as the reason for this Frenchiness had to do with the history of Richard, I must tell you a little about him before going on with the boys.

One hundred and thirty years before, Richard's great-grandfather, William, Duke of Normandy (which was part of France), had got together an army and sailed over and conquered England, to which he claimed a right, and had made himself king. The Saxons who lived there had fought hard, but had to submit; and King William and the Norman knights who had come with him, though they settled down to live in England, for a long while still spoke their own French language and did things as they had done in Normandy.

When William died his children and grand-children grew up and married into noble French families, dukes and counts of large domains, so that by the time that Richard became king of England he had inherited also at least half of France. And though he was not called king of these French possessions but, as was the custom of the time, had to render "homage" for them to King Philip, nevertheless the latter knew that the homage was scarely more than a form; and as Richard grew more and more powerful, Philip became more and more uneasy lest he gain possession of still more of France. At the same time Richard on his part more than suspected that Philip, who was crafty as he himself was open, was trying to get from him his French inheritance.

So it was that though they had once been good friends they had come to distrust one another, and odd as it may seem, that was one reason why they had gone together on the crusade. Neither wanted to go away and leave the other behind for fear his kingdom would be gone when he came back. Yet while they disliked and suspected each other, for the sake of the success of the crusade they tried to work together and of course always behaved most politely.

And now that we understand more about the kings, let us go back for a minute to the history of our boys. Hugh's father, Sir Kenneth of Alnwyck, was of Norman descent and had been a friend of King Richard in his youth; his mother was a Saxon lady, and though from her he had learned the language of England, French was usually spoken in the home which was a beautiful castle on the banks of the river Wye. But Hugh had not lived there since he was seven years old, for, as was the Norman custom, boys of that age were always sent away to the home of some other noble knight to be brought up and trained. They spent the first seven years in their new home as pages, then at fourteen they became squires, and finally, at twenty-one, if considered worthy, they received knighthood. So Hugh had been sent to the castle of an English knight, also of Norman blood, where he had lived happily for five years, learning many things not in books, of which there were but few then.

Meantime the boy's father had suffered a long illness which had left him quite helpless; and when he heard of the crusade King Richard was planning he was broken-hearted at being unable to take the cross himself and go along, for he was a brave knight. But remembering his friendship for Richard, whom he had seen much of in Normandy long before he was king, he had sent word to him begging that he would take Hugh with him as page. Sir Kenneth felt it would comfort him to know at least that his young son was going, if only as a page, and that he might do some service in the army of the cross. For the wish to be a crusader was taking everybody by storm. King Richard, to the joy of both Hugh and his father, had readily granted the latter's request; and the lad had shown himself so bright and mannerly that he had already become a favorite with his master.

Raymond's history was, in part, not unlike that of Hugh.

His father, a baron of Languedoc, had sent him to be trained in the chateau of his friend Count William de Pratelles; when Count William joined the crusaders, as of course no knight could take with him all the pages and squires he had at home, he had chosen Raymond because of his faithfulness and obedience.

So now we are ready to go on with our story again. As I said before, the boys found much to interest them, and whenever they had a spare moment they spent it together poking around the great camp. One morning when thus looking about, "The big fighting machines are all put together," said Hugh, "and do you see that roof of fresh hides on the tall wooden tower? A soldier told me that it was soaked in vinegar and that the Greek fire couldn't burn it!"

"Is that so?" said Raymond, looking with interest at the great tower–like structure built in several stories and mounted on wheels so that it might be loaded with archers and drawn up close to the walls of the besieged city. For King Richard, in spite of his sickness, had ordered the machines he had brought with him to be set up, a fort to be bult and preparations made so far as possible for the attack on Acre which he hoped to make as soon as he was able. "Just see how far along the new fort is," went on Raymond. "I wonder how the Acre people like the looks of it," and he glanced toward the battered city walls where the Saracen flag still flew with its crescent and single star.

As the boys strolled along it was like going through a

great tented town. Everywhere were flying the banners and pennons of innumerable knights, and here and there were war-horses being groomed or hounds blinking in the sun. Armorers were busy looking over the long tunics of metal, or "hauberks," as they were called, some made of hundreds of rings of steel sewn on thick leather, some of small metal rings linked together like a chain purse, and some of scales of steel lapping over each other. Then there were curious helmets of all kinds being rubbed up. Some of these were of chain mail like the hauberks; but most were round with flat tops, looking much like kitchen saucepans turned upside down. Lances and spears and bows and arrows were everywhere to be seen. And everywhere, too, were crosses. Each man wore his cross of red cloth on the breast or sleeve of his tunic, unless he belonged to one of the military orders, in which case it was fastened on the shoulder of a large black or white mantle, and he wore a red cap with a white one under it and carried a staff tipped by a small white shield bearing a white cross.

There were two of these military orders, or societies, one called the Knights of the Temple and the other the Knights of St. John; both having been started in Jerusalem a long while before and their object being to try to protect pilgrims from the Saracens. They had begun simply as brotherhoods of monks, though all were of noble birth. The Knights of the Temple, so named because their house was near the temple in the holy city, would go to the coast whenever pilgrims landed and do their best to fight off the Saracens, who would often attack them; the Knights of St. John, or Hospitallers, as they were often called, took care of those who fell sick or were wounded in these fights. The two orders had been small and poor at first, but had grown so rich and powerful that when the crusades began both took an important part in the fighting, and in the camp at Acre their tents and banners covered a large space.

Beyond these were three small churches built of wood, for as many of the crusaders had been there so long they had tried to supply some of the things they had had at home. And as they were not fighting or praying all the while, they found ways to amuse themselves between times. They had laid out lists and sometimes tournaments were held, where the noble knights fought in sham battles (as if they did not have enough real ones!) while the ladies looked on; for there were a number of the latter in the camp. There were troubadours who sang songs, and storytellers and even jugglers to entertain when there was a lull in the fighting. Often, too, some of the knights would make bold to mount their war-horses and gallop off with their falcons on their wrists to chase hawks or other birds. For this kind of hunting was a sport all delighted in, and many had brought with them their finest falcons, which were natural birds of prey and had been carefully trained to chase and capture other birds. Indeed, as the boys reached the edge of the French camp, a horseman attended by two squires dashed past with a smile of greeting for both lads. "There goes Count William hunting!" cried

Raymond. "Did you see his falcon? It's a beauty. I feed and tend it. Did King Richard bring his?"

"Bring his?" echoed Hugh. "Well, I should think so! He's brought his favorite, named Arrow, and a dozen besides. I believe he'd as soon think of leaving his head behind, for he likes hawking better than almost anything else in the world except for fighting and playing on his lute and making up poetry; you know he's great at that. He keeps the lute near his bed where it's always handy, and the falcons are in the tent just beyond his, and I help take care of them."

Here the boys fell to discussing the training of falcons, till presently they found themselves at the moat which I told you the crusaders had been obliged to dig around their camp to help protect them from the Saracens camped beyond and ready to attack them from behind and so distract their attention whenever they tried to assault the city. As now the boys looked across the deep ditch filled with sea water, the Saracen camp, like that of the crusaders, seemed a town of tents. There were fewer fluttering banners and pennons than those of the Christians, but many of the tents were striped with gay colors and gorgeously furnished within. Indeed, if our two pages could have peeped into that belonging to the Sultan Saladin, camped with his hosts on the hills beyond the city, they would have fairly gasped at the magnificence of it, for the people of the far East have always loved color and gold and gems, and Saladin's tent was much more splendid than even the handsome ones of the crusading kings.

But though Hugh and Raymond could not see all these things, they could watch the strange people moving about in their gay robes. Darkeyed Egyptians in brightly striped mantles and turbans; tall, swarthy Nubians from the desert, in white robes and with heads swathed in many folds of white linen; brown Arabs sitting by their tents polishing long spears, or else rubbing down the silky coats of their swift-footed horses; all these were a never ending wonder to the boys.

Then from where the camp stretched far out they could hear the cries of the many people who came daily to sell their wares. There were donkeys laden with fagots, water-carriers with goat-, some even with ox-skins full of water, for any fit to drink was scarce in Palestine, and so were bottles and barrels, so this was the way it was carried about and sold; there were sweetmeat and fruit venders, all shouting at the top of their voices, dogs barking,—but all at once Hugh, who had been eagerly watching as much as he could, caught sight of something he had never seen before. "What's that queer beast over yonder?" he cried, "See! it has *humps* on its back!"

"Oh," said Raymond, smiling, "that's a camel. You'll see lots of them here; they carry things on their backs, and people ride on them."

"I can't imagine how!" said Hugh, still gazing; for there were no circuses then so folks could know about the animals of far countries.

If the boys could only have walked through the camp they would have found many more things to interest them.

They would have seen bakers, always a pair of them, sitting cross-legged by the queerest ovens, just square holes in the ground, a couple of feet wide and deep, and lined with smooth, hard plaster. One of the men would be throwing in bundles of dry thorn-bush, which, blazing up quickly, would make the plaster very hot. Then the other baker, who had been patting out large round loaves of dough, scarcely thicker than pasteboard, would clap them one by one on the sides of the over where they would bake in a minute or two. Beyond these perhaps would be a barber sitting on his heels while his customer, whose head he was shaving, knelt on a rug before him.

Then there were fortune-tellers, and letter-writers, in flowing robes and with long ebony cases for their reed pens stuck in their girdles, writing letters for soldiers, beginning each at the back of a folded sheet of parchment and writing in slanting lines toward the upper lefthand corner, so filling every page to the front of the sheet, where the letter ended. Why did they write backward like that? Dear me! I do not know, except that their ancestors had always done so, just as, when reading their books, they began at the back and read toward the front, instead of the way we do. If our boys could have looked into some of the finer tents they likely would have seen men seated on cushions, their slippers with curled-up toes on a rug beside them. If meal-time, they would have in front of them little tabourettes, tiny round tables not more than two feet high, with large brass trays on them set out with bowls of food and baskets of fruit. What kind of food? Well, except the fruit, mostly things you would not like: mutton or kid cut up in chunks and boiled with all sorts of queer flavors; curdled milk, lentils and rice, maybe, all of which they ate with their fingers. Where were their plates and knives and forks and spoons? They did not have any! Instead, each man had beside him a pile of the thin round loaves the bakers had made; taking one of these he would double it over and use it to scoop up the meat and gravy, everybody eating from the same bowl. Did not their fingers get frightfully sticky? Of course, but then, when they finished, a servant would bring a handsome copper ewer and basin and pour water over their hands and dry them on a napkin. But that would not have been a strange sight to our pages, who were used to serving their masters the same way; for nobody used forks then and the crusaders' fingers got as sticky as anybody's.

Nevertheless there were so many odd things going on it was a pity the two boys could not get a closer glimpse of them. They did see a good deal though, and a crusader soldier who was standing near, guarding the moat, noticing their interest, pointed out some more. "Do you see that long, low roof over yonder?" he asked; and as the boys looked, "That's a big bazaar where they have all kinds of queer things to sell. And over that way," pointing in another direction, "they have a regular market, and they are always trying to get things across the moat here and through our camp into the city. Only last night our archers shot down a boat-load of them, and I guess their stuff is pretty salty by this time!" and he smiled grimly as he glanced down into the water beneath.

"They've got a regular bath place, too," he went on, "and a mosque over yonder for their heathen worship. I can hear those outlandish-looking priests of theirs every day when they call out 'La Allah! La Allah!' or something like that, and then you ought to see all those folks drop down on their knees as quick as lightning and begin mumbling prayers to some of their heathenish gods! Pah! the dogs of infidels!" and the soldier spat on the ground to show his contempt for the whole Saracen race.

And no doubt at the same time, over in the enemy camp, there were Saracens who looked across the moat and spoke of "the dogs of Christians" with their little wooden churches. No doubt, too, the Saracens understood the Christian worship as little as the soldier did theirs, and were just as contemptuous when every evening crusaders bowed their heads in prayer as a loud-voiced herald went through the camp shouting out "God save the Holy Sepulchre!" Later on both Christians and Saracens came to know each other better and to look with more respect on the efforts of each to seek God;—but it took a long time.

Meanwhile our two boys had turned away from the moat, and "Let's go over where Queen Berengaria's tent is," said Hugh. "Maybe there will be a puppet show to see."

"All right," answered Raymond, and they scampered off toward the ladies' quarters, for there was generally amusement of some kind going on there.

CHAPTER IV
Assaulting the City

One morning as Hugh was moving quietly about, putting his master's tent in order, the sick king, lying on his bed with closed eyes, slightly roused and asked the two faithful knights watching by him, "Does Philip attack the city soon? I thought I heard my squires whispering about it."

"Yes, Sire," answered one of the knights, "the French army will assault Acre at mid-day."

Richard only shrugged his shoulders and again closed his eyes. But when Hugh, having finished his work, stepped outside, he heard other knights talking. "It's too bad King Richard can't do anything!" said one. "Yes," replied the other, "you know he is still desperately sick, but King Philip doesn't want to wait, and some of the English troops will help guard the moat."

And this reply of the knight showed one of the reasons why the crusaders did not get along so well as they might. There was more or less jealousy between the armies of the different nations, and they did not always work together to the best advantage. When the French made an attack, part of the English would often hold back, and the French would do the same way when the English king led. And Duke Leopold of Austria was often sulky and wouldn't fight with the others. The crusaders might have won much more than they did, if they had all rallied round one leader, as did the Saracens, who obeyed every command of their great Sultan Saladin.

So now a part of the English waited for Richard to get well and lead them, though quite a number of others made ready to help guard the moat. Hugh, who was not then needed in the royal tent, ran after these as they rode toward the edge of the camp. Meantime in the French section Raymond was hurrying about as fast as he could, waiting on the squires of Count William as they armed him.

Of course while all these preparations were being made to attack the city, the people shut up there had been watching from the walls and had not missed anything. Suddenly a deafening noise arose, and Hugh, running toward the moat, turned around and rushed nearer the Acre walls, where the din was growing louder and louder. "What's that noise for?" he asked breathlessly of a French soldier who had stopped to fasten his helmet.

"Oh," said the soldier, "that's the signal the Saracens make to tell Saladin's troops and all those Egyptians and Arabians yonder that we are going to assault Acre. Then they will try to cross the moat and attack us from behind, and of course that always takes a lot of our men from fighting to get into the city. Just hear those infidels beating their drums and banging and pounding on anything that will make a noise! Some of them even pound on brass and copper cooking pots and platters!"

Sure enough, as the soldier had said, Saladin's troops heard the signal and rushing down from their camp on the hills joined their allies beyond the moat, and soon the din of battle drowned the noise in the besieged city, for at the same moment the French army began a furious assault. Dragging up their huge battering-rams, they thumped and pounded the great walls; from the petraries and mangonels heavy stones were hurled against and over them, and from archers on the ground and others stationed in tall wooden towers wheeled up close to the city flew an incessant shower of arrows.

Hugh, who had found a group of pages busy carrying fresh arrows to these archers, at once began to help too and almost ran into Raymond eagerly hurrying to bring a shield to one who had dropped his. Then the boys scampered to a sheltered nook behind one of the petraries, for they had no armor and showers of arrows and stones and Greek fire were pouring down from the walls, which the Saracens were defending with a desperate bravery. Hugh noticed that the rams were battering hardest of all against one tall tower in an angle of the wall, and "Look!" he heard one of the men shout as he helped work the huge wooden beam, "The old Cursed Tower shook that time!" For this was what the crusaders had named it, and they all especially hated it and wanted to knock it down, because it was said to have been built with the thirty pieces of silver which Judas received for betraying our Lord Jesus.

But though it shook, the Cursed Tower did not fall; and

though the French knights fought valiantly it was in vain they tried to scale the massive walls they could not batter down; for so deadly was the Greek fire poured upon them and so fiercely did the Saracens resist, that at last they were forced to retreat, having lost many of their number. Moreover, the fighting at the moat had been so violent that a large number of the crusaders had been obliged to leave the city walls and go there. All were bitterly mortified, especially as the Saracens, seeing them retreating, began to jeer from the walls and to taunt them with cowardice; which was not true, for the bravest fighters in Christendom were in the crusading army. But to take a strongly walled city in those days was not an easy task. Fever had weakened many of the crusaders, their heavy armor was a burden under the burning sun of Palestine, but worst of all, the quarrels and disagreements of their leaders made it hard for the army to make headway.

King Philip was so disappointed over the defeat of his effort that his fever came back for a while, so with both kings sick in their tents, the besieging army settled down to comparative quiet. That is, they delayed making another assault, but at intervals, every day and night, the big battering-rams pounded away, and now and then a shower of stones would be hurled over the walls by the other machines. Hugh and Raymond were much interested in these, especially one that belonged to the French army and that Philip had named "Bad Neighbor."

"Do you see," said Hugh one day as they were watching

this send a huge stone into the city, "the Acre people have set up a petrary on top of the wall almost as big as Bad Neighbor?"

"Yes," said a crusader coming with his arms full of stones, "and do you know what the heathen call theirs?—'Bad Kinsman!'"

Here, "Hark!" cried Raymond, "that's a herald! Hear his trumpet?"

Everybody stopped working the fighting machines and stared at a queer little procession coming through the camp. "Well, what's that?" exclaimed Hugh in bewilderment; but as nobody could tell, both boys hurried off to find out.

"It's an English herald!" said Raymond as they ran along.

"Yes," said Hugh, "and there's a big Saracen behind him carrying a white flag, and then come six black men with white turbans, some bringing baskets, and some goatskins like the water carriers do in this country."

The tall, dark figures, looking neither to right nor left, followed the herald who cleared a path for them, announcing that they came on a peaceful errand from the Sultan Saladin. Straight on they went toward the quarters of King Richard, seeing which, Hugh sprang after them and flew as fast as his legs would carry him to his master's tent, reaching it just as the strangers disappeared with in one close by.

Raymond, who had hurried after him and was waiting near by, hoping Hugh would come out and tell him the news, soon began to hear the soldiers talking, for nothing was long kept secret from the camp. "Well! If that don't beat everything!" said one. "They say that heathen Saladin has sent cold sherbets and the finest fruit to 'The Malek Ric!'"

"Who's that?" asked a soldier who had not been long with the army.

"Why, that what those Saracens call King Richard, 'Malek' is their heathenish name of king, and I suppose 'Ric' is as near as they can come to Richard. It's got to be a sort of nickname for him here."

"That Saladin can't be such a bad fellow," replied the other. "I heard my master say the other day that if he would turn Christian, he would make a fine honorable knight."

Here Hugh came out of the tent, and Raymond, knowing nothing had escaped him, ran to him, asking, "Did Saladin really send things to King Richard?"

"Yes, indeed!" answered Hugh. "They wouldn't let anybody in the king's tent, but took them to the one near it and I got right by the door and saw it all. Those goatskins were full of sherbet packed in snow from the top of the mountains, and the baskets heaped with the finest fruit you ever saw! The black men were slaves from Nubia, and their leader brought a message from the sultan saying he was sorry 'The Malek Ric' was sick and that he didn't want him to die like a slave in his tent, but to get well so he could fight him in the open field. And he said he'd send him dainties every day till he was all right. The herald interpreted for them; you know he can speak their langue."

"Whew!" exclaimed Raymond, "wasn't that fine of Saladin!"

as Hugh paused, enjoying his importance as news-dealer, for others had gathered around to listen.

"Yes," he went on, "King Richard was mightily pleased when one of his knights went in and told him, and he sent a message of thanks to the sultan and ordered presents given to all the slaves. And then I heard that he drank a cup of the sherbet right away to show his contempt for the opinion of some of the knights who thought the things might be poisoned. He said Saladin might be an infidel, but he was as honorable as any knight in our army."

And this was quite true. Both Saladin and Richard were brave fighters and generous foes and greatly admired one another, though they had never met; and it really seemed a pity that fate had made them enemies when in many ways they might have enjoyed each other's friendship.

CHAPTER V
The Fall of Acre

Of the two kings whom we left in bed in the last chapter, Philip, who was least ill, crept out first and turned his attention to the building of more fighting machines, besides seeing that Bad Neighbor was kept in repair, for it was often broken to pieces by Bad Kinsman, which had the advantage of hurling stones from the high wall. Richard also, who was slowly recovering, though unable to be up, was having more machines got ready, and the two pages never tired of watching their progress. Always, too, some parts of the city walls were being battered by different sections of the army.

"I don't see how those walls stand so much pounding!" said Raymond one morning as the two boys were looking on.

"I don't either!" replied Hugh. "The Duke of Burgundy and Duke Leopold both have their machines going today, and when I came out of King Richard's camp the Knights of the Temple were dragging theirs around to the other side of that old Cursed Tower."

Here the boys passed close to a great wooden stone-throwing machine at one side of which stood a priest in black robe droning out, "God save the Holy Sepulchre! Come up and pay your pence for the Petrary of God!" For this was the name of

HUGH RAN FORWARD AND PULLED UP THE DART.

the machine, which had been built at the common expense of the whole army; and always the priest stood there to preach and collect money to repair it when damaged by the enemy. The two lads had gone only a short distance beyond this when suddenly they sprang back with startled exclamations as an arrow whizzed past, a few paces in front, and buried its point in the earth. Though they had been warned not to go too near the city walls, they had grown rather reckless, and now they glanced up sharply to see if any more were coming; but as the sky seemed clear, Hugh ran forward and pulled up the dart still quivering in the ground.

"See!" he cried in surprise, "it has a folded piece of parchment fastened to it, and something written on the outside of it!" He and Raymond screwed up their faces and examined it with puzzled eyes, till at last, "Pshaw!" he said, "what's the use! We can't read it! Let's take it to the priest yonder; he ought to be able to!" For there were no regular schools in those days and, aside from monks and priests, few people, even those of noble rank, could read or write.

The boys hurried over to the Petrary of God and showed the carefully folded bit of parchment to the priest, explaining to him how it had come. The priest, after making out the direction on the outside, did not venture to unfold it, but holding it tightly in his hand, said, "This is evidently a message to the king of England, for his name is written on it. It is strange who could have sent it in such a way from the city yonder."

"Well," said Hugh impatiently, "give it to me, and I will take it to him."

"Not so fast, boy," answered the priest, "such a message as this is too important to any stray lad. We must find some trustworthy soldier."

At this Hugh's face flushed, and drawing himself up proudly, "Sir priest," he said, "I would have you know I am no 'stray lad,' but one of King Richard's own pages. Here are his three leopards worked on my sleeve!"

The priest, who did not see very well, now looked Hugh over more carefully and knew from the leopards the boy spoke the truth, for no one not in the service of the king would dare display them. So, handing the parchment to him with "Well, well, boy, I meant no offense," he went on with his droning "God save the Holy Sepulchre!"

Hugh, scowling darkly, received the message and the two boys set off at a run for the English camp, where, at the royal tent, they delivered it to one of the knights attending the sick king; then they hung around, waiting for any news that might leak out, as news generally did. And before long Hugh learned from one of the squires that the parchment really was important. The squire thought it gave valuable information that would help Richard plan his attack on the city.

"Who sent it?" asked Raymond.

"Nobody knows!" answered Hugh. "King Richard was as surprised as anybody."

And it certainly seemed strange that, though every day or

two fresh messages, always directed to King Richard continued to arrive in the camp in the same way, no one ever found out who was the sender. It has always been thought, however, that it was some Christian captive in Acre who in some way contrived to shoot the arrows over the wall and who dared not sign his name lest, if found out by the Saracens, he should be killed. At any rate the information thus gained was a great help to the crusaders.

By and by the continual battering of the rams began to tell. The machines of Philip broke down a small part of the wall and the Petrary of God knocked off a corner of the Cursed Tower; yet the armies were unable to enter the city. Meantime Richard, though still too weak to walk, was growing restive, and one day when Hugh went into his tent to carry a basket of fine Damascus plums from Saladin, he found the king sitting on the edge of his bed while two squires were trying to comb his tawny hair and beard, snarled from his long tossing with fever till they stood out like a lion's mane.

Just then, as one of them struggled with a hard tangle, the king made a wry face, and "Hugh," he said, "come here and be my barber. These varlets are pulling me unmercifully!" and his eyes snapped dangerously. The squires, glad to be released, handed the ivory combs to the page, who, though rather frightened at the task, was deft-handed and managed successfully to smooth out the tangled locks. Then he brought a copper basin and ewer of water and helped his master wash, and the knights and squires attending him dressed him in his linen tunic, cross-gartered his hose from knee to ankle, and put on his soft leather shoes. When Hugh saw them bringing out his hauberk of chain mail and helmet, "Why, he is not going to try to fight, is he?" he whispered in surprise to one of the squires.

"Not exactly," answered the squire, "but he's given orders to attack the city today. Our sappers are to try to undermine the wall, and if they can make a big enough break in it, there will be a general assault, and King Richard is to be carried on his bed to the new tower so he can direct the men. Run over to the pile of cushions yonder and bring an armful."

Hugh quickly obeyed and brought the cushions, which he helped arrange so the king could partly sit up; then, all being ready, four knights took up the corners of the silken-covered bed and carried their royal master out of the tent and up the steps of the new fighting tower he had had built. His bed was placed on the topmost of its four platforms, the roof of which was spread with raw-hides steeped in vinegar to protect it from fire. The tower was then filled with the best English archers and rolled near the city wall. As Hugh watched he could see that under it crept men dragging huge logs and all kinds of shovels and mining tools; and as soon as they were near enough they began digging as hard as they could under a part of the wall by the Cursed Tower. As the hole grew bigger they propped up the earth over their heads with the great logs.

Meantime, the Saracens, not dreaming that Richard himself

was in the tower or that their wall was being undermined, merely supposed that the attack of the archers was part of the day's work to which they had grown used. To be sure, their archers sent down showers of arrows in return, but if one showed himself an instant from behind the parapet, down he tumbled, the mark of some English bowman. Presently, when one appeared on the wall wearing the armor of a knight whom he had killed the day before, Richard's eyes flashed, and seizing a cross-bow near his bed, he sent an arrow straight into the Saracen's heart. The king was an expert with the cross-bow, and one after another a dozen or more of his shafts flew, never one missing its mark.

While this was going on the petraries and rams had not been idle, and were banging the Cursed Tower as the sappers, having set fire to the logs in their hole under the wall, crept hurriedly out. In a little while, when the logs had burned through, there was a great crash as down fell the Cursed Tower, and the walls settled into the hole, leaving a wide breach. At this there was a loud shout from the crusaders, and the English knights and foot-solders who had been waiting rushed to the assault.

But the Saracens, too, rushed to defend themselves, and fierce and terrible was the battle. Hand to hand they fought, the swords and battle-axes of the crusaders dealing deadly blows, the archers sending their arrows in clouds, and all the while the petraries and catapults hurling their great stones into the city.

But though the crusaders fought bravely, so did the Saracens, and they had one weapon which nothing could withstand, the terrible Greek fire. They had prepared a fresh supply of this, and poured it down mercilessly on the besieging army till at last the crusaders were forced to fall back.

Hugh and Raymond, who had been anxiously watching the battle, drew long faces as they heard the trumpeters give the signal for retreat. "Oh!" said Hugh, "I thought surely they would get in this time!"

"So did I!" answered Raymond. "I believe they could if our army had helped. I don't see why they don't work together more!"

Here four knights came bringing King Richard on his bed, and Hugh ran to the tent. He was surprised, though, to see that as the king was carried in he did not look down-hearted, as he had expected, but that he seemed much brighter. The fact was, Richard knew that the day's work had destroyed enough of the wall so that the crusaders could not long be kept out, and that the Saracens themselves must realize by this time how determined a foe they had and that they might as well surrender.

And this was just about what happened. The Saracens, though they had once more forced the enemy to retreat, knew their own strength was spent; they knew also that the crusaders, while not entirely united, might any day make up their disputes and attack in a body, when they could not hope to withstand them; and worst of all, their scanty supply of food was now entirely gone, and Richard's ships and army kept such close watch that no more could be brought to them by sea or smuggled in by land. So, worn out by their two years' siege, they sent messengers to Saladin begging him to allow them to surrender, and at last he reluctantly gave his consent.

It was a gaunt and sorrowful procession that marched out of Acre, carrying nothing with them save the clothes they wore. And it was a battered and wretched city they left behind, though it was not entirely empty, as it still held over two thousand Christians whom the Saracens had kept captive through all the long siege. The crusaders made it their first work to care for these, and then they strove so far as possible to clean and purify the city before the entrance of the army, which was to take place a week or more later.

CHAPTER VI

On the Road to Jerusalem

Ten days after its fall, the crusading army made its grand entry into Acre. By this time Richard was again able to ride Favelle, and as usual he led the procession. Kings, queens, and knights, all were magnificently dressed, and even the common soldiers had freshened up their tunics and polished their spears and shields so they looked very fine as they streamed through the crooked streets of the dingy old city. Hugh and Raymond, following their masters on foot, gazed curiously around at the queer flat-roofed houses of stone or plaster, all showing heavy doors, and their few windows closely latticed.

Richard soon established himself, with the two queens and their attendants, in the largest of the stone houses. It had been the palace used by Saladin when in Acre and was built around a courtyard where had once been a beautiful garden; tall palms and cypress trees still rose from it, but the flowers were withered and neglected, for water had been too scarce in the besieged city to spare any for them. Like most houses in Eastern countries, the palace proved much handsomer within than you would have supposed from the plain wall without; but it was not furnished like the castles Hugh was used to at home, and as he followed his master to his room he looked in vain for chairs or beds, or tables. What did they sit and sleep on? Why, divans built against the walls and piled with cushions. Were there tabourettes to eat from? To be sure; handsome ones, inlaid with pearl and ebony and silver, and trays with fine porcelain bowls and tiny coffee cups in holders of filigree gold and silver. And everywhere were magnificent rugs and curtains. Hugh helped bring his master's belongings to him, and placed his own in a little alcove near by.

Meanwhile, King Philip was not at all pleased to put up with a second-best place; while as for Duke Leopold of Austria, he was cross and sulky as could be because he was obliged to take what was left, for, stupid and conceited as he was, he thought himself quite as good as any king there; and, to prove it, that very evening he had his banner set up on the tower where floated those of Richard and Philip.

Next morning, Hugh, who had risen early, heard a commotion in his master's room. Richard was not yet up, but already one of his knights had brought him word, "Sire, Duke Leopold's banner is mounted beside your own!"

That was enough for the Lion Heart. *"What?"* he cried. "Dares the impudent Austrian swine insult us so?" Then rising up to his bed, "Hugh!" he called, "Quick! Bring me water and comb!" For he had taken a great notion for Hugh's help at his toilet. Hugh hurried to serve his master, who, with further aid from his squires, was soon dressed. One of them insisted on bringing him some bread and wine, which he quickly dispatched; then he strode from the house toward the tower, followed by a little party of knights, all anxious to see what he would do.

Hugh ran along and watched to tower as the king mounted the winding stair and came to the parapet where the banners floated. With a low growl as of an angry lion, he seized Duke Leopold's, and tearing it from its place, flung it down and set his foot upon it. Everybody drew a long breath as he coolly came down the stair and returned to his quarters.

Later in the day, when the two pages got together as they usually managed to, they talked it over. "They say Duke Leopold is furious!" said Raymond. "Yes," agreed Hugh, "but he knows well enough he'd better keep away from King Richard. It was fine the way he tore down that Austrian rag!" and Hugh's eyes snapped, for he was proud to serve the Lion Heart, whose reckless boldness and bravery he ardently admired. Some of Richard's knights, however, were not sure he had done well to trample on the banner as he did, for though Duke Leopold did not dare to do anything then, they knew him to be a sullen, resentful man, who would nurse his wrath and bide his time to do the king an ill turn. And Richard, though warmly loved by a host of admiring friends, nevertheless, by his proud bearing and contempt for those he disliked, had made numerous enemies among the crusaders, who could ill afford to add to the many quarrels among themselves.

But though the older people kept up their disputes, the two pages continued the best of friends and every day found some chance to explore the old city together. In ordinary times its narrow, crooked streets would have been crowded with just such noisy throngs as had gone daily among the tents beyond the moat. But now the boys could peer into the dark, empty little booths that served for shops, and into the deserted mosques; these were the Saracen churches, each with a domed roof, and beside it a tall, slender tower circled high up by a balcony where every day their priests had many times called the people to pray to Allah, which was their name for God. The dwelling-houses all had their flat roofs protected by low walls or little wooden fences, and looking at these one day, "Those house-tops are queer," said Hugh, "but they surely are a very good plan for a warm country like this."

"Yes, indeed," said Raymond, "and Count William says that the people in Palestine often eat and sleep and do all sorts of things on their roofs when they are shady in the mornings and evenings. And they are splendid places to see anything going on in the street." Sometimes the boys climbed the battered city walls and looked down at the camp, where the common soldiers were still quartered, and at the blue sea beyond them and the green mountains behind.

Thus the crusading army rested for about three weeks, when more trouble began to brew. This time it was the lack of real friendliness between the two kings that began to be whispered about more boldly, though almost from the fall of the city it had been hinted at. And soon everybody knew the trouble. King Philip was going home! Hugh could hardly believe his ears when he heard one of the squires say so. *"What!"* he exclaimed, "going to leave the crusade? How *dares* he?"

"Well," said the squire, "crusade or no crusade, that's what he is going to do. I was talking with some of the French soldiers, and they have their orders to get ready to go."

"But *why?"* asked Hugh in amazement.

"I guess he don't tell all his reasons to everybody," said the squire, "but he says he is sick and that he is needed at home. But the soldiers seemed to think it's more because he's out of sorts with King Richard and doesn't like to take second place, as he generally has to." And the squire smiled, for the Lion Heart's followers all liked his high-handed way of doing things.

That afternoon Raymond came running to the nook by the Cursed tower, where the boys usually met, looking very woe-begone. "Hugh", he burst out, "isn't it dreadful that King Philip is going home?"

"Yes, indeed," said Hugh, "and will he take all the French with him?"

"No," replied Raymond, "it seems the other crusaders made such a fuss he has to leave ten thousand men under the Duke of Burgundy, and thank goodness, Count William is one of them, so I won't have to go!" For the lad was really very much mortified that his king should desert the cause, and would have been heart-broken had he been compelled to follow him. And Hugh also was delighted that he would not have to part from his friend.

Sure enough, a few days later the French king and the greater part of his army took their leave. As the ships sailed out of the harbor there came a sound of hissing from the troops on shore, who felt themselves deserted without reason; and they had to realize that to conquer the Holy Land was a thousand times harder task than they had supposed. But Richard watched in silent scorn; there was a far-away look in his eyes and, as the last sail disappeared, the smouldering fire in them seemed to leap to little tongues of flame. He was deeply and bitterly disappointed in the action of Philip; morever, he was sure the latter had more reason than jealousy for going home and that he meant to scheme to get his French possessions away from him, though he had solemnly promised to do nothing unfriendly while the crusade lasted. But Richard said no word of this, keeping his thoughts to himself. And as to the crusade, though no one saw more clearly than he the difficulty of the task, he still hoped that he might be able to take Jerusalem if only he could get enough soldiers. So to this end he sent messengers on the returning ships to try and gain more men from his English and French dominions.

Meanwhile, he gave orders for the host still in Acre to make ready to start for the holy city, for he knew that it would be a long march, and thought that if more soldiers came from home they could join them on the way. But to get things ready to move was no easy matter; for many of the men who had been besieging the city longest had grown lazy with their rest within it and lost their enthusiasm for going farther; and Duke Leopold and his Austrians were surly and unmanageable because Richard was now the head of the crusade. However, after many delays, all was finally arranged. The two queens and their ladies were to stay in the palace at Acre, a garrison was left to guard the city and at last late in July the crusaders set out, and in spite of all their troubles looked very brave and gay.

The white surcoats and red crosses of the knights gleamed in the sunlight and their fluttering banners were as bright as a garden of flowers. Behind these came the foot-soldiers marching in solid columns, then the great baggage-wagons, beside which were grouped the pages of the various knights. Hugh and Raymond walked together, though when the army paused for food and rest or to camp at night they separated to find and wait upon their masters. Then at the end of the whole body of troops was always a guard of soldiers to protect them from attack behind. King Richard had arranged also that a fleet of ships should sail along as the army moved and supply it with food.

Thus the crusaders started off over the sands and beneath the hot sun that was soon to make their armor an intolerable burden, though they dared not cast it off because of the con-stant shower of arrows that day by day fell upon them from the Saracen hosts. For back of the long line of hills, which ran parallel to the narrow strip of coast, Saladin led a great army, moving as the crusader moved. These hills were beautiful with groves of olive and fig and citron trees, and here and there shone the gold of oranges, but the soldiers of the cross had little time to look at them, so busy were they watching for the flying arrows. Though Saladin's men outnumbered Richard's three to one, he did not wish to risk an open battle with the latter, but hoped rather to wear them out by his bands of archers, who would dash out on their swift Arab horses, shoot their volley of arrows, and rush back at a wild gallop.

"Goodness!" cried Hugh, as a shower of darts fell on the men just ahead of them as the marched along one hot morning, "they have so many arrows sticking in their chain armor, they look like porcupines!"

"I don't think many are hurt who have good armor," said Raymond, "but some who haven't are hard hit! I'm thankful we have the big baggage-wagons between us and the hills yonder!"

"Our cross-bowman seem to do more damage with their long bolts when they can get a chance at those heathen, but their Arab horses are so fast they're gone before you know it!" said Hugh.

"Well," said Raymond, "they must have plenty of arrows to waste! They are fairly paving the ground with them. I'm tired of tramping over them!"

"They're not so bad as tarantulas, though," answered Hugh. "Look out! There's one now!"

Raymond jumped aside as Hugh, spying a stone, promptly

dropped it on the great spider. These tarantulas, and scorpions, too, added much to the hardships of the soldiers, often creeping into their tents and wounding them with poisonous bites. Indeed, as the crusaders toiled on day after day beneath the scorching sun, they found more and more discomforts to bear. Many at last tore off their heavy armor and threw it away, preferring to risk the Saracens' arrows rather than endure it longer. Often their feet were torn and bleeding from the low-growing thorny bushes through which their way led; and always they must watch for some sudden move of the enemy; for though Saladin did not want to risk a big battle, many were the whirlwind attacks his followers made on the less protected parts of the army. At such times, when King Richard would hear of it, he would gallop furiously along the lines, hurling his lance and wielding his great battle-ax, and always then the Saracens, shouting, *"The Malek Ric!"* fled before him as fast as their Arab horses could carry them.

At last the army neared Jaffa, and the two pages toiling along with the rest were glad. Raymond, limping a little from a thorn in his foot, listened as Hugh said, "I heard the folks around King Richard's tent talking last evening, and they said we'd reach Jaffa in a couple of days, but that tomorrow we have such a narrow strip of coast to march over that our army will have to string out, so maybe the Saracens will dare attack us more boldly; but the king, while he wants an open battle, doesn't want one to begin till we get to a better place to fight."

"I heard pretty much the same thing in Count William's tent," said Raymond. "I guess everybody is warned to be on the watch tomorrow."

Sure enough, that night, after the herald had cried through the camp "God save the Holy Sepulchre!", the word was passed around that no battle was to be started on the morrow until they heard King Richard's signal, two blasts on the trumpet, blown three times.

Next morning the boys were all excitement as the army started off. The king led as usual, and after him rode the Knights of the Temple' behind these came the long line of crusaders, both on horse and foot, while guarding the rear along the narrow coast, soon they came in sight of the beautiful gardens around a town named Assur. "Oh, look!" cried Hugh, gazing at the wilderness of roses and jessamines and laden fruit trees of every kind, while shining among them were ripe oranges and lemons and scarlet pomegranates, and towering overhead rose clusters of stately palms. But scarely had the boys begun to admire all this, when suddenly such a storm of arrows broke over the rear of the army, and even the baggage-wagons, that the two pages had to dodge to keep from being hit.

It was as King Richard had guessed. The Sultan Saladin had decided to make a bold attack at that spot, hoping to drive the crusaders into the sea. He had began on the Knights of St. John, as being farthest from the fiery Richard. The knights chafed and fretted under their orders not to fight till the signal was given and sent a messenger galloping to the king begging permission to charge the Saracens, but Richard sent back word to wait for his signal. Thicker and thicker fell the arrows, till at last the brave knights could bear it no longer, and with a loud shout, "For Saint George and the Sepulchre!" they dashed headlong at the foe.

The battle thus begun, though sooner than Richard had planned, he at once took the lead. The baggage column and the pages, being ordered to keep out of the way, drew off to one side of where the main fight was raging. Hugh and Raymond, aching to be in it, were obliged to content themselves with climbing on top of one of the loaded wagons and looking on; and so fearful a sight it grew that for a little while they stared in utter silence, though the din of battle was so great that they could scarcely have heard each other speak, had they tried. Led by the brave Saladin, on rushed the Saracens, pouring from the defiles of the hills with the most frightful cries. They seemed to think the more noise they made the more terrifying they would be. They beat on brazen drums, they blew on great trumpets, they shrieked and yelled as they swept on, white men, yellow men, brown and black, from the different countries that Saladin ruled. Gorgeously dressed in many stripes and colors and with heads wound with white or gay turbans, there seemed no end of the host from behind the hills. But the crusaders were ready for them. Raising their own war-cries and meeting them fearlessly, knights and foot-soldiers stood their ground bravely, dealing terrific blows with their heavier weapons.

As the boys watched breathlessly, presently, "Look at King Richard!" cried Hugh. But Raymond was already staring with all his might as the Lion Heart, mounted Favelle, dashed furiously to and fro through the fight, fiercely swinging his battle-ax and cutting a wide path before him as he went.

"Did you ever see anything like him?" again exclaimed Hugh. "You can fairly see the blue fire darting from his eyes, and he mows down the Saracens like wheat in August. See how they fly before him!"

"He is simply terrific!" replied Raymond. "We saw some pretty stiff fighting around Acre, but King Richard was sick then. I didn't know anybody *could* do things like that! Why, if all the soldiers were like him there wouldn't be a Saracen left alive!"

Indeed, with all his daring exploits and fame for bravery, never had Richard deserved the name of Lion Heart more truly than as he dashed headlong through the battle Assur, dealing death with every blow, and all the while so skillfully directing the movements of his army that in the end the Saracens were utterly defeated. Those who remained of Saladin's great host, leaving their thousands of slain heaped upon the shore, fled terror-stricken to the refuge of the hills.

The losses of the crusaders were few compared to those of the enemy; and when the dead and wounded had been cared for, they made their camp around the walls of Assur, where they were to rest for a day. Richard's tent was pitched in the midst of the beautiful gardens which luckily had been beyond the battlefield, and Hugh gathered some of the choicest fruit from these and brought it on a silver salver to refresh his master after the hard-fought struggle of the day.

CHAPTER VII

The King Goes Falconing

It was now October and the crusading army had been ten days at Jaffa. They had found the walls broken down and much of the city destroyed; for Saladin, discouraged by his defeat at Assur, had not tried to hold the place, but rather to make it as little use as possible to Richard. But the latter, as soon as the soldiers had rested a little, had set them to work repairing the broken walls so the city might be a safe place for his ships to land their food.

Hugh and Raymond and all the other pages, whenever at leisure, helped carry mortar and wait on the men. The work was going well, and one bright morning King Richard decided to take a day's sport with his falcons. A small party of English and French knights, including Raymond's master and a few squires attending them, went along. When they were ready to start, at the king's command, the boys ran to the tent where the royal falcons were kept and supplied those of the knights who had not brought their own birds from home. Hugh handed up to his master his favorite, Arrow, who sat proudly on King Richard's wrist. As was the custom for falcons, his head was covered with a tiny hood so nothing might distract his attention till some hawk came in sight and he was loosed to chase it; Arrow's hood was of purple velvet tipped with a gold tassel and he held his head very high as he rode along.

After the party was gone, the two pages explored the old city for a while, then went and hunted shells by the seashore; and when the afternoon was nearly spent they sat under a fig tree by the road, eating its fruit and watching for the return of the party.

As the boys talked and watched, the sun slowly sank in the west, and as dusk fell, others besides themselves began to look anxiously for the sportsmen. But it was quite dark and the torches had been lighted for some time in the camp before the falconers rode slowly into Jaffa. As a crowd of knights gathered about them they saw their pace had been slow because some of them were wounded. Everyone could see that King Richard was silent and troubled; and when Raymond ran to attend Count William he could not find him anywhere.

One of the squires, noticing him, said, "If you are looking for Count William de Pratelles, he is not here."

Raymond stared at him a moment in blank amazement, then, "Where is he?" he cried. But the squire was already following King Richard, so the lad hurried along with Hugh and turned into the courtyard of the large stone house where the king lodged. When Hugh sprang to hold his master's stirrup, "Lad," said King Richard, "bring writing materials to my room at once."

Hugh hastened to obey, and soon fetched the tip of a cow's horn, set in silver, that served as inkstand, a quill pen and sheet of parchment; and the king, without waiting for rest or food, at once began to write. When he had finished and Hugh had brought wax and a lighted candle so he might seal the letter with his royal ring, the page's next errand was to find and bring to the house a trusty messenger whom the king named. To him Richard gave the letter and a large purse of gold, ordering him to take the swiftest horse in camp and seek Saladin as quickly as possible. As soon as the messenger was gone, "Hugh," said the king, "now get me a basin of water and send in a squire to brush the dust from my tunic."

When the page and squire had helped their master freshen up, they brought him food and drink. Then, bidding Hugh hand him his lute, he dismissed them, and soon they could hear soft, plaintive strains of music and the echo of a song. For no matter how troubled over the happenings of the day, the Lion Heart could always comfort himself thus, or, best of all, by the making of a new song, which he could do wonderfully well.

Meantime, out in the courtyard a group of eager listeners had been hearing an account of the hawking party, from another of the squires, and this is what he told them: "Things went all very well at first. We rode along a little stream and started two or three herons and a hawk and the king and knights flew their falcons and had fine sport. Toward noon the sun got pretty hot, and we saw a wood ahead of us and rode into it and spread out the lunch we had brought. Afterward there was a little more sport, and then most of the party were rather tired and were for turning back; you know how this climate is,—you can't do things the way you can at home.

"King Richard, though, wasn't ready to go back; he told the rest they could stay there and he would ride on a bit and see if he could start another hawk. You know how bold he is and never thinks of any danger to himself. But no sooner had he set off than count William de Pratelles—"

Here Raymond could keep still no longer: "Oh! Is he *dead?*" he asked, his eyes full of tears.

"No, lad," answered the squire, "at least I hope not; but let me go on. As I was saying Count William, and a few of the other knights and a couple of us squires got on our horses and followed after, though the king did not see us. Pretty soon he spied a hawk and set Arrow loose and galloped ahead to see the chase, so fast we could hardly keep him in sight.

"At last, when Arrow had killed the hawk, even King Richard seemed tired, and getting off his horse, threw himself down under a tree and went to sleep as coolly as if there wasn't a Saracen within a thousand miles. He slept an hour or more, and the afternoon was getting on, and we knew it would take a while to ride back to Jaffa, but nobody liked to wake him.

"In a few minutes, though, it was done for us. A party of Saracens suddenly burst out of a thicket and rushed on the king. At that he jumped up, half awake, and sprang on his horse and began slashing down with his sword. Of course we all hurried up to help him, and everybody began to fight hard, though none of us had anything but swords. King Richard disposed of at least seven of the Saracens single-handed, when the rest pretended to fly. But it was only a muse to draw us into ambush, for they had probably been watching our party from the start. Anyhow, we had chased them only a little way when a big group of heathen galloped out of the deep woods and surrounded our little handful of men, far outnumbering us.

"We were in a pretty bad fix, fighting against so many to one. King Richard, as usual, inched away furiously with the sword."

"They seemed to be trying to take him prisoner and it looked as if nothing could save him, when suddenly Count William, in the thick of the fight, seeing how things were going, put on a disdainful air as if surprised that the heathen didn't know him, and called out—you know he can speak their barbaric tongue—that *he* was 'The Malek Ric!' At this they left King Richard and rushed on *him*, which was what he meant them to do, for he wanted to save King Richard: and the infidels took him prisoner and rode off so fast we couldn't tell where they had gone."

Here the squire paused a moment, and a murmur of admiration for Count William rose from the listeners in the courtyard when they realized the noble sacrifice he had made; for everyone knew he was likely to be beheaded by the Saracens, who showed little mercy to prisoners. Poor Raymond, when he heard his master's probable fate discussed by those about him, was not ashamed to burst into tears, for Count William had always been good and kind to him and he loved him much.

But the squire went on: "There isn't much more to tell. King Richard had been fighting so hard he knew nothing of what Count William had done till it was all over, and then he was hot for pursuing the Saracens no matter how many. But by this time it was dark and, besides, the heathen had scattered and gone in different directions, so nobody knew which way the prisoner had been taken, and there was nothing left to do but come back here." Everyone was talking of what had happened when Hugh hurried into the courtyard after being dismissed by King Richard, and he soon learned the squire's story from Raymond, who could not repress a bitter sob as he thought of his master's probable cruel death. Hugh tried to comfort him as best he could, and, "Come, stay here with me," he said; "we can sleep together, and I'm sure King Richard will be glad to have you."

Raymond was glad to accept the offer, and later on, when the boys went to the little room where Hugh slept, they talked long. Hugh knew enough to hold his tongue about his master's affairs except those he was sure would make no difference to tell, and so had said nothing to anyone in the courtyard about Richard's letter to Saladin. But now an idea occurred to him, and knowing that Raymond, too, could hold his tongue, he told him of the letter and purse of gold. "I wondered at the time," he said, "why he was in such a hurry and what it was all about, but I believe now he sent the messenger to try to ransom Count William. And they say that even if he is a heathen, Saladin is such a gentleman and admires King Richard so much that I think he won't have Count William killed, but will let him be ransomed."

Raymond quite took heart at what Hugh told him, and both, feeling much relieved, soon went to sleep. And indeed, Hugh had guessed exactly right as to what Richard had done.

CHAPTER VIII

Malek Adel Visits Richard

When the Saracens who had captured Count William brought him, a few days later, to the sultan's camp, and he was found not to be "The Malek Ric" as they supposed, they were angry and wished to behead him at once. This Saladin was quite willing they should do, and it was only the prompt arrival of the messenger, who had ridden at full speed, that saved him. For on reading Richard's letter, Saladin at once granted his request to ransom Count William.

The latter had given himself up to die, and great was his joy when, with a courteous farewell, the sultan dismissed him and even sent some of his own soldiers to escort him safely back to the crusader's camp: for when not actually fighting, both the king and the sultan and the nobles in both armies were chivalrous enough to behave most politely to one another.

Of course on his return, more than a week after his capture, Count William received a warm welcome, and Raymond was delighted to have his master to serve once more. Count William was surprised, however, to find the crusaders still resting in Jaffa, for he knew the king was anxious to go on.

The two pages also used to wonder why they delayed there. They could not know how hard Richard had tried to move the common soldiers, many of whom had grown lazy, as at Acre, with the easy life at Jaffa. Nor could they know all the jealousy and opposition he met with from the leading knights, the Dukes of Burgundy and Austria, and even the chiefs of the Knights of the Temple and of St. John. And most difficult and irritating of all was a great quarrel going on between two powerful nobles, Conrad of Montferrat and Guy of Lusignan, as to which should be called king of Jerusalem; which seemed particularly silly, as Jersualem was yet to be taken by the crusaders and the task looked every day more impossible. Nevertheless, Conrad, who had a large number of followers, was very angry because Richard favored Guy's claims instead of his own, and it was even said that he had turned traitor to the cause and offered to join his forces with Saladin in fighting the King.

But though our pages could not know all of Richard's troubles, the camp was full of rumors of them; and everyone knew that a messenger had come from the sultan to arrange a meeting between the latter's brother Malek Adel (which means King Adel), and King Richard, and that it was to talk about possible terms of peace. For Saladin thought perhaps the English king might now be willing to listen to such.

On the day Malek Adel was to come, Hugh helped carry his master's royal tent to one of the finest gardens outside the walls of Jaffa. When all was ready and Richard, handsomely dressed and attended by a group of knights, including Count William, waited for his visitor, Hugh went out, and soon joined by Raymond, the two sat in the shade of a pomegranate bush and watched the road from the hills. Presently a party of horsemen came in sight; as they drew nearer, "Look!" said Hugh, "that one in the middle must be Malek Adel! What a splendid purple mantle all glittering with gold! And what gorgeous trappings all the horses have on!"

"And see!" cried Raymond, "there comes a string of camels, seven of them? Do you suppose they are a present?"

"I guess so," replied Hugh, as the boys sprang up and stood ready for any service. Hugh had hoped to hold the bridle-rein or stirrup of Malek Adel as he dismounted, but as he and the two nobles with him were attended by their own Nubian slaves there was nothing for the pages to do but look on as the English king, stepping to the door of his tent, received his visitors with the utmost courtesy. After this greeting Malek Adel presented to King Richard the camels he had brought, and directed a slave to unroll a package from the back of one of them. This second gift proved to be a magnificent silken tent, which King Richard at once ordered to be pitched in the garden so all might see its beauty. After it had been duly admired, and the party had entered the royal one already prepared for them, at a signal from one of the squires Hugh went in and passed around sherbet and fruit and sweetmeats on silver trays.

When he was dismissed and joined Raymond again, "Those Saracen lords certainly are good-looking," he said, "and my! such splendid robes and turbans and mantles! You know

King Richard likes handsome clothes himself, and I'm glad he had on that brocaded mantle of his and one of his best embroidered tunics."

"What do you suppose he will do with all those camels"? asked Raymond.

'I don't know," said Hugh. "They might carry his baggage on the march, but they look so fine with their red harnesses and all those little silver bells and gay saddle cloths that I don't believe they're meant for anything but riding on, and of course that wouldn't suit King Richard."

Meantime, while the boys were talking, much more important affairs were discussed within the royal tent. But though, when Malek Adel left, no peace terms had been reached, nevertheless a warm friendship had sprung up between him and King Richard, and after that day it was no uncommon sight for the Saracen king to visit his English foe, with whom he found many tastes in common. And more than once, at these times, Hugh brought his lute to King Richard, who played and sang for Malek Adel; and though the latter was not himself gifted to do the same in return, he sometimes brought with him the most skilful of the Saracen poets and musicians to perform for King Richard's pleasure. Some of the crusaders did not like this friendship, but the king treated their opinions with his usual contempt, and when it came to battles neither he nor Malek Adel fought a whit less fiercely because they liked each other.

Indeed, no one should have criticized the Lion Heart for

KING RICHARD, WHO PLAYED AND SANG FOR MALEK ADEL.

finding a little pleasure where he could, for troubles were thickening around him fast enough. One day when the pages were together, "I tell you," said Hugh, "I'd hate to head this crusade! The knights are fussing about this and that, and if you hear the common soldiers talk, they will say in one breath that King Richard ought to lead them right away to Jerusalem and in the next that it's a shame to make them move till they get rested. Rested! Why, we've been here weeks now! They say King Richard has a hot temper, but I think he's been mighty patient with it all!"

But at last the army was got together, and leaving a force to guard Jaffa, they set out for Jerusalem, though they little guessed the many hardships in store for them. It was now Novemeber, and a season of heavy storms was beginning. As our two pages trudged day after day along the muddy roads, they were often glad to climb up on the baggage wagons to shield themselves from the driving rain that drenched them to the skin. When the camp was made at night, tents were blown over and everything soaked, or the tired soldiers tormented into wakefulness by the enemy. For the Saracens, moving as before behind the hills, had a way of sending a small force galloping toward the crusaders' camp at night and yelling at the top of their lungs; then, when the crusaders rousing up, would spring to arms, off they would gallop again. And no matter how often this happened, King Richard's army never dared not to get up and arm, as in the darkness they could never be sure how many were attacking them. And this was just what Saladin wanted, for in this way most of his soldiers could sleep peacefully in their tents while King Richard's were kept worried and fagged and quite worn out when daylight came.

Soon, too, their food began to fail. The provision ships, which had followed them down the coast, could not land because of the storms; Saladin had caused the country through which they passed to be laid waste, and the rains spoiled the food they carried with them. Hugh and Raymond, though for the first time in their lives they suffered real hunger, were proving good soldiers and said nothing as they munched their mouldy bread and drank the muddy water from the scanty streams they passed; for most of the wells had been poisoned. No wonder that many of the crusaders fell sick and died, and many more could scarely bear the weight of their armor, which every day the rains rusted more and more. And the poor horses suffered as much as the men, for in the desolate fields it was almost impossible to find fodder for them; many fell exhausted by the way, and the famished crusaders did not disdain their flesh for food. Thus, hungry and thirsty and footsore, the army toiled painfully on till at last they camped at a place called Ramlah.

Every day, as Hugh had waited upon his master, he had found him more silent and troubled, even his lute seeming scarcely to comfort him. Indeed, as the tents were pitched at Ramlah, though hardly more than fifteen miles from Jerusalem, King Richard knew in his heart that never had the holy city seemed farther away. That evening, after Hugh had carried his scanty supper to him, the king bade him bring a map he had lately caused to be made of Jerusalem and the country round about. Hugh placed the roll of parchment on a table and by it a lighted candle, and left King Richard poring over it, as he continued to do half the night. When at last he laid it aside, a deep sigh broke from the Lion Heart as with sad shake of his head he threw himself down for a few hours' rest.

The next morning, when Hugh went in to wait upon him, "Lad," he said, "you need not help pack the tent things today. We are going no further now."

Hugh gasped, but as King Richard turned around with an air of dismissal, he went outside and sat disconsolately on a rock, wondering what the king meant; and thinking miserably, too, of the good breakfast they would be having in his far-away home castle and how empty his own stomach was, how damp and uncomfortable his clothes were, and how tired he was most of the time now. Soon he pricked up his ears, as a herald rode through the camp calling out that the army would not go to Jersulaem then, but after resting two days at Ramiah would march to the city of Ascalon to wait for reinforcements.

When the herald ceased, at first there was a blank silence, and then from the foot-soliders rose a great murmur of discontent. As Hugh got up and walked among them he heard them talk. "What!" said one, "Retreat now, after all we have suffered? For shame!" "Yes," cried another, leave the Holy

Sepulchre now, and have to endure hunger and cold and misery marching to Ascalon instead of Jerusalem? And who knows when reinforcements will come?" "No", went another, "I don't believe there will be any!"

By the next day the discontent grew worse, and many began to desert. In the afternoon Raymond came over to where Hugh sat huddled from the rain under a flap of the royal tent. "What do you think?" he said. "A lot of the French are going off with the Duke of Burgundy! Some have already started. But Count William is loyal to King Richard and says he doesn't see how he could lead the army further now, it's so worn out. And on the way here I heard some other knights say that spies the king sent ahead brought back word that Saladin had made the walls of Jerusalem so strong it will be mighty hard to take."

"Yes," replied Hugh, "I know King Richard has a new map of the city. He was looking at it nearly all night, and I guess that decided him to give up the march now. But I don't believe anybody feels worse about it than he does. He looks dreadfully sad and worried."

It was in truth a terrible wrench for the Lion Heart to give up, if only for a time, the object for which he had sacrificed and toiled and suffered so much. But he was too great a general not to realize that the odds were against him; he had done his best, but now he must have help. Deserted by King Philip, his army torn by quarreling and worn by hunger, thirst and sickness, he could not hope to conquer the strong city of their dreams. He would not give up altogether, though so he had plannend to march to Ascalon and there wait for the reinforcements he had sent for long before and which he still hoped would come. Besides, Ascalon was one of the last of the important places on the coast, which the crusaders had not taken, and holding it, they could land ships with men or food almost anywhere needed.

The march thither was full of all the hardships they had endured before, only worse; for now came snow and hail, too, and Hugh and Raymond had to wrap their little woolen capes closely about them to try to warm their numb fingers. All were thankful when at last, early in January, Ascalon came in sight, though they saw that, as at Jaffa, Saladin had caused the city walls to be broken down and many of its houses destroyed; but enough were found still unharmed to shelter the king and chief knights, and as usual the two pages made themselves useful helping arrange things for their noble masters.

CHAPTER IX

The Old Man of the Mountain

King Richard had hoped to find some of his food ships at Ascalon, but though a number were on the way there, several had gone to the bottom in the hard storms and the rest were unable to land. Every day Hugh and Raymond went down to the wharf, hungrily watching for these ships, but it was over a week before they could sail into the harbor. "Good!" cried Hugh, who first spied them, "There they come! I hope they have plenty on board! I feel as if I could eat a whole sheep and several loaves of bread all by myself!

"So do I!" answered Raymond, as they ran to see the vessels unload.

When everybody had enough to eat again and had rested a little from their hard march, they were much better humored, and King Richard set himself to work to coax them to make up their many quarrels and be friends; for he knew that unless all the crusaders were united they could never hope to capture Jerusalem. He even sent messengers to ask the Duke of Burgundy to come back with all the French troops he had taken away, and this the jealous duke at last consented to do.

The next thing King Richard undertook was to rebuild the broken walls of the city, and as these were very large he knew it would take a long time unless everybody helped; so he commanded all, from the noblest knight to the commonest foot-soldier, to go to work, setting the example himself by seizing a trowel and mixing up mortar and starting to lay stones as hard as ever he could. Count William went to work near the king, and soon nearly everybody was busy, Hugh and Raymond hurrying about helping mix and carry mortar, and often laying some of the smaller stones themselves.

The army had been working thus for several days when Hugh said to Raymond, "Seems to me everyone who is able is working on these walls except those Austrian soldiers and their Duke Leopold. I'd like to know what's the matter with them and if they think they're any better than King Richard and the rest of us!"

"Look!" said Raymond. "There comes Duke Leopold now! I wish King Richard would do something to him!"

And Raymond was not disappointed: for just then the Lion Heart, working at a gap in the wall near by, glanced up and saw the duke as he strolled idly along. "Halt!" cried the king instantly, as his eyes flashed. The other, staring, paused sulkily. "Now, sir," said King Richard, "get a trowel and go to work like the rest of the army!"

But Leopold only tossed his head and replied haughtily, "I am the son of neither a carpenter nor a stone mason that I should work like a common laborer!" With this he tried to pass on, but Richard was too quick for him. Without another word he pounced upon him, and seizing the proud duke's burly shoulders, thrust him out through the gap in the wall, helping him along with a sound kick. Everybody near looked on open-mouthed as the king, calmly picking up his trowel, went on with his work as though nothing had happened.

Hugh and Raymond, peeping through the gap, could hardly keep from laughing as Leopold, amazed at finding himself thrown out of the city, and afraid to touch the Lion Heart, at last gathered himself together and stalked off in a towering rage. "Of course King Richard has been trying to keep things peaceful," whispered Hugh, "but I guess that stupid Duke Leopold was just too much for him! You know how he detests him!"

"Yes," said Raymond, "and I don't blame him! I suppose Leopold will go home now, but I don't think he or his Austrians will be much loss."

Evidently Richard thought the same way, for he gave orders for the duke and all his followers who were lodged in the city to camp outside the walls they would not help build, for he said they had no right to any protection from them. And as soon as they could get ready to leave, they set off for Austria as fast as they could go, Leopold still raging and biding his time to pay King Richard back.

Day by day the broken walls rose higher and higher; though Richard looked in vain for the reinforcements he longed for. Saladin, too, camped as usual behind the hills, was waiting for fresh troops, and there was a truce between the two armies. As was their custom when not really fighting, the king and sultan behaved to each other with the greatest friendliness; and as the weather grew better toward spring, the armies would often have parades and tournaments, in which the knights and nobles of both sides took part. As the two pages were watching a tournament one day, "Doesn't it seem funny," said Raymond, "how friendly everybody is between fights?"

"Yes," replied Hugh, "and the sultan and King Richard give each other lots of presents, all kinds of things. I'm glad when I see Saladin's black slaves coming to the door, for they always bring something pleasant, and that's more than can be said for the Christian messengers who have been coming lately."

"What do you mean?" said Raymond. "Well," said Hugh, "a messenger came from England a while ago, and another one yesterday: they bring big parchment letters all covered with wax seals, and when King Richard reads them he looks worried to death. I'm sure he has been getting bad news from home."

And this was quite true. Richard had been getting the worst kind of news from home. Letters from his mother and friends urged him to return and save his kingdom, which his own brother John was trying to get away from him. They told him also that King Philip, in spite of his solemn promises to do nothing against Richard while he was away, had broken his word and invaded Normandy. All these evil tidings were hard for the Lion Heart to bear after all his misfortunes and suffering in the Holy Land. He was really in a very trying position. Though he had never lost a battle, everything had gone against him. He could not bear to go away and leave Jerusalem unconquered; neither could he afford to lose his kingdom. Then too, if he returned to England, he knew he must leave some leader strong enough to hold what the crusaders had already won; and Richard could not but admit that the man who could do this best was Conrad of Montferrat. You remember this was the Conrad who was disputing with Guy of Lusignan about being king of Jerusalem. The quarrel had been going on for months, and everybody took sides one way or another. Indeed, if any crusader had nothing else to start a quarrel, he could always succeed by beginning to argue about Guy and Conrad. For though the walls of Jerusalem were still unshaken, all still hoped that they would soon take the city; and if they did, of course it would be very important to be its king.

Richard thought it over, and at last, though much against his will, decided to allow Conrad to be called king of Jerusalem; for he could not be crowned without Richard's consent. He despised Conrad's treachery in offering to join Saladin, but felt sure that if he won in the quarrel with Guy, he would come back to the crusaders, whom he could hold together better than anyone else. Richard decided also to make up for Guy's disappointment by giving him the island of Cyprus, which he had taken away from King Isaac on his way to Acre. He then made his plans to return to his kingdom and overcome his enemies in England and France so that he might start another crusade; for he could not give up hope of some day conquering Jerusalem.

Having made up his mind, Richard sent his nephew, Count Henry of Champagne, sailing up the coast to the city of Tyre, of which Conrad had made himself master, to tell him he was to be crowned king of Jerusalem. It was very ridiculous that he had to be crowned in Tyre because the city of which he was called king was still held by the Sultan Saladin; but nobody seemed to see it that way.

When the camp knew Richard's decision, there was a great deal of discussion. They were still talking about it when, scarcely two weeks later, there came sailing into port the same royal galley that had taken Count Henry to Tyre, and a messenger quickly landed and hurried to the quarters of the king. Having delivered his message first to Richard, he came into the courtyard, and soon all there knew the word he brought, for it was no secret. Conrad, before he could be crowned, had been killed by the order of The Old Man of the Mountain. Before long the whole camp had heard it, and if tongues had wagged before, now they were buzzing twice as busily.

Hugh was burning with curiosity and longed for a chance to ask the messenger more; so he was glad when presently food was made ready and he was sent to bid the man into the house and serve him while he ate. The moment he had finished, "Sir" he said, "will you please tell me who is "The Old Man of the Mountain?""

"Gracious!" exclaimed the messenger, "have you just come to this country that you have never heard of him?"

"No," said Hugh, "I've been here a good while, and I've heard his name and asked the soldiers about him once or twice, but they seemed almost afraid to talk of him, so I never found out much."

"Well," replied the messenger, "nobody knows so very much about him. I guess because nobody wants to go very near to find out. All the crusaders call him 'The Old Man of the Mountain,' but the Saracens, who know more than we do of the heathenish people over here, say his real name is Senan, and that he is chief of a tribe called Ismaelians, who live up on Mount Lebanon. They say he has a splendid castle up there, with wonderful gardens and fountains, and that he has gold and jewels and clothes and things to eat fit for a king. And no wonder, for he has had enough people robbed and killed to get most anything he wants."

"Mercy!" cried Hugh, "can't anybody stop him?"

"No," said the messenger, "that's not so easy. He's no ordinary bandit, and he doesn't do the work himself, either; he's too high and mighty for that. They say he takes boys from the tribe and trains them in his castle till they grow up, and he gives them a queer kind of drug that makes them do anything he tells them to. So if he orders them to kill anybody, they will surely do it, if it takes them years to get a chance. Everybody in this country knows a man's life isn't worth a fig if the Old Man of the Mountain wants him put out of the way. So you see it isn't so easy to get rid of The Old Man. It's not like fighting an open battle; he does everything so secretly, and has so many people to obey him, that nobody who makes an enemy of him knows what minute he may have a dagger thrust into him as Conrad did."

Hugh shivered. "Did he rob Conrad?" he asked.

"No," said the messenger, "he doesn't always kill for robbery. People in Tyre think there was some quarrel between them. And what do you suppose The Old Man did? Six months ago he sent to Tyre two of the young men he had trained, and they were ordered to kill Conrad. They disguised themselves as monks, pretended they were good Christians, and made friends with some of the best people in the city, all the while watching for a chance to get at Conrad."

"Did nobody suspect them?" asked Hugh.

"Not a soul," replied the messenger. "They went to church and behaved so piously that everybody thought they were all right."

"How did they get Conrad at last?" again asked Hugh.

"Well," said the messenger, "it was the night after Count Henry came, and Conrad and his friends were tremendously pleased that he was to be king of Jerusalem. The Bishop of Beauvaise gave a fine dinner for him, and as he was riding back to his house, suddenly the two false monks sprang at him, stabbing him with their daggers so he fell dying from his horse." Hugh shuddered again, and said, "Did they catch the young men?"

"Oh, yes, to be sure," replied the other, "the people around soon caught them, and made short work of them without much trouble. The Old Man of the Mountain tells all his followers that if they lose their lives in obeying his wicked orders, they will go straight to Paradise and have the grandest kind of a time. And the miserable wretches believe everything he says, so when they have carried out his commands, they don't seem to mind it at all if they get killed themselves."

Here the messenger got up and stretched himself. "Well," he said I suppose King Richard will have to pick out another king for Jerusalem. Meantime I must go aboard the galley, for we are to sail back to Tyre whenever he gives the order."

That night, when Hugh went to bed, he dreamed of disguised monks and Old Men of the Mountains till he was thankful to wake up and find himself still alive and the sun shining.

CHAPTER X
The Hill of Hebron

It was now May, and in the gardens of Ascalon the peach and apricot trees were laden with young fruit, while the roadsides shone with scarlet anemones and golden poppies. The crusading army, rested and no longer hungry, took cheer; but all the beauty around him could not comfort the troubled spirit of King Richard. The news from home was still as bad as ever, but he had been obliged to put off his return there for another year. Even before the death of Conrad the crusaders had been unwilling for him to leave them, and he felt he could not do so now. For though he had chosen Count Henry of Champagne to be called king of Jerusalem, he knew that if left to head the crusade, the count, with all his bravery and loyalty, lacked power to settle the hard questions that were always coming up.

And one of the hardest of these was worrying Richard right then. The army was demanding to be led once more to Jerusalem; And while of course the taking of the city and rescue of the Holy Sepulchre was the great thing for which he had come, he knew far better than the rest how impossible it was to hope to do it then. The reinforcements he had waited for had not come, though Saladin's army had all the while grown bigger and stronger. Richard foresaw that while the crusaders, full of fresh hope and courage, might start again for the holy city, as they drew near they would find the same hardships they had found before, and they would have neither the strength nor numbers to attempt a long siege of its strong walls. When a leader so bold and of such heroic bravery as the Lion Heart hesitated to undertake the thing he most cared to do, the rest of the crusaders should have known he had the best of reasons. But they would listen to nothing, and at last declared that if Richard would not lead them they would go by themselves.

At this the king yielded, though against his own judgment; perhaps he thought the only way was to let them find out for themselves how it would turn out. At any rate, having decided to go, he made preparations with all his usual energy. Hugh was sent flying here and there on many errands, provisions were got together, knights rode out to gather in the straggling foot-soldiers, and when all was ready, one bright Sunday morning they set off.

As our two pages marched along together they could not help but feel full of hope and cheer. For the first week or more the country was green and flowery, they had plenty to eat, fresh streams to drink from, and, best of all, the crusaders, happy in being once more on the road to Jerusalem, seemed to have laid aside their quarrels for the time and showed each other the greatest kindness. "There!" said Hugh one morning, "that's the third knight today I've seen get off his horse so a sick foot-soldier can ride it!"

"Yes," said Raymond, "and haven't you noticed how the rich share their money with the poorer ones in the army so they can buy things they need? Everybody seems to be trying to be as good as they can!"

But this pleasant state of affairs did not last long. As they went farther and farther from the seashore, so the ships could no longer supply them, food again became scarce, for it took a great deal for so many men. As they drew nearer Jerusalem, again they found the whole country laid waste, not even providing enough for the horses, while the streams failed and no one dared to drink from the poisoned wells. And the hungrier and thirstier they became, the harder it was to bear the heat of the Palestine sun. Hotter and hotter it blazed, till, as before, many fell sick and died, while still more began to straggle off and desert.

At last, after the greatest hardships and suffering, the worn-out army managed to reach Hebron, this time only seven miles from the holy city. That sounds very near, but to Richard with his famished and footsore men it seemed a long way yet; and seeing the utter hopelessness of it all, he determined to camp there a few days, until he and the chief knights could decide whether to go on, for he wanted them to see for themselves how matters were.

Hugh, as he attended his master on the march, had seen each day how more and more troubled he grew, and as they camped there at Hebron his heart fairly ached for him. When he carried in his supper, which Richard scarcely touched, he found him sitting with his head bowed on his hands, and as he raised his fearless blue eyes that had been so full of high hopes and dreams, the lad could not but be struck with the disappointment and misery in them. Indeed, one can only guess what the lion-hearted king must have suffered, knowing at last that he must give up the dream he had cherished for years, for which he had worked and planned and fought, had sacrificed his fortune and almost his kingdom. Bitter, bitter must have been his thoughts of Philip, who had deserted him, of the quarrels and misfortunes that had divided and dimished his army, and the thousand and one things that, in spite of all his boldness and courage and military skill, now forced him to leave Jersualem still unconquered, the Holy Sepulchre still in the hands of the infidels. For he knew that the knights whom he had asked to help him decide whether to go on must at last agree with him that it was quite hopeless.

The next day a group of soldiers were talking and Hugh heard one of them say, "I saw one of the spies the king sent ahead to get news of the city,—you know he sent out spies the other time, too,—this one came back this morning, and he says the walls of Jerusalem are stronger than ever. It seems last winter, while we were waiting for reinforcements, everybody from the sultan down worked on the walls, just as King Richard and the rest of us did at Ascalon. Saladin even brought stones for them on the back of his fine horse; and as the walls were tremendously strong to begin with, now nobody could take the place, except maybe by a long siege, and we are in no shape for that!"

"I should think not!" said another standing by. "We would starve to death ourselves long before we could starve out those heathens by a siege!"

"They say Saladin has an enormous army," put in a third, "and if we tried to besiege the city with our few men, he could swing around behind us, and then where would we be?"

For even the common soldiers now could begin to see some of the things Richard had foreseen at the beginning of the march. And when the knights he had called together talked over everything, they agreed, as he knew they must, that it would be death for the army to try to take the city. Like many crusaders before and after them, they had at last learned the bitter truth that to conquer Jerusalem was a task to baffle the boldest, and a thousand times harder than it had seemed to their eager hearts as they had set off from their far-away homes. And hardest of all it was to give up their dream of rescuing Christ's tomb when they had marched almost in sight of it!

Indeed, only a few miles from Hebron there was a hill from which Jerusalem could be plainly seen. The afternoon of the day it was decided to turn back, Richard ordered Favelle to be brought to his tent door, and Hugh held the bridle while he mounted; and then, attended by Count William and a few other knights and squires, he rode off in the direction of this hill.

"Do you suppose they are going to look at Jerusalem?" asked Raymond, who had run over to talk to Hugh.

"Yes," said Hugh, "I think Richard wants to see it even if he has to give up taking it. Oh, isn't it just a shame the way things have turned out! I had no idea when we started that a crusade was such a hard thing!"

"Neither had I," replied Raymond, "and I do wish we could go on,—but," he added with a sigh, "it would seem mighty nice to have enough to eat again, and all the fresh water we want to drink! I'm sick of these muddy, brackish brooks around here!" for he was very thirsty.

"So am I," agreed Hugh, "and sick of eating dead horses!" for he was very hungry.

"I wish we could go over that hill and see the city," said Raymond.

"We could walk the few miles easily enough," replied Hugh "but we wouldn't have time today before they got back, and they might want us for something. But likely we can find a chance tomorrow."

A few hours later, when Richard and his party returned, Hugh ran to take Favelle, and the king walked into his tent with such a far-away look in his eyes that he seemed not to hear as the knights took leave of him. The next morning both the pages asked permission, which was readily granted, to go to the hill, though Hugh was puzzled at King Richard's answer when he inquired if one could really see the city from there. "So they say, lad," replied the king absently, with such a strange expression in his face the page dared not ask more. But when he and Raymond set off together, "Raymond," he said, "didn't they go to look at the city yesterday?"

"Yes," answered Raymond, "but what do you think Count William told some knights who came to the tent last evening while I was fixing his bed? He said that as they rode toward the hill the king hardly spoke a word, but seemed thinking things over all to himself. Then at last, when they reached the highest point, from which he says you can see the city quite distinctly, one of the squires, who had been there before, led Favelle to the best place to look at it, and they all reined their horses to one side so as not to interfere with the king's view. And then, while they waited for him to take the first look, King Richard—he had been riding with his head bowed—made as if he would raise his eyes, then suddenly he dropped his head again and lifted his shield before his face. You know they all wore their armor and had their swords and shields along."

"What?" exclaimed Hugh, *"didn't he look at all?"*

"No," replied Raymond, "that's the strange part of it. It seemed as if, when it came right to the point, much as he wanted to see Jerusalem, he couldn't quite stand it. Count William, who was nearest to him, said he heard him say in a low tone, as if talking to himself, something about how, since God had held him unworthy to conquer the city and rescue

"LIFTED HIS SHIELD BEFORE HIS FACE."

the Holy Sepulchre, he felt himself unworthy to look at it. Anyway, still holding the shield before his eyes as if he was afraid he might look in spite of himself, he turned his horse around and quietly waited till the others had seen what they wanted, and then rode back without another word."

Hugh was silent a few moments, and then he said slowly, "Well, that was just like him. You know, besides being a tremendous fighter, he's a poet, too, and I've heard that poets feel things like that more than other people. He must be frightfully disappointed, especially as he hasn't been beaten in a single battle here. It's just that everything else has gone against him!"

As the boys talked they were all the while going along as fast as they could, and before long had reached and climbed the hill to its highest point. But as they stood with eager eyes gazing on the distant city of Jerusalem, the chatter on their lips died away. The towers and domes shone in the sunlight, and the great walls girdling the city about showed how strong a fortress it was. In all the long months, almost a year, since they had landed at Acre, every night the hearld had cried through the camp, "God save the Holy Sepulchre!"and now, somewhere within those frowning walls on which they looked, was the tomb for the sake of which they had toiled and suffered so much; and boys though they were, the two pages could not help but feel their hearts swell as there swept over them the great pang of disappointment which all the crusaders shared.

CHAPTER XI

The Battles at Jaffa

It was July, 1192, a year from the coming of the crusaders, and Richard was again camped at Acre, this time on his way home. He had skillfully and safely led the retreating army from Hebron back to Ascalon, though pursued and many times attacked by great forces of Saracens. From Ascalon they had made their way to Jaffa, where the sick and wounded, who were many, had been left in care of the garrison and the Christian inhabitants of the place; then at last they had come to Acre, whence the greater part of the army had already sailed northward for Beirut. For though Richard had not conquered Jerusalem, he had taken and held all but one of the important cities along the coast; this last, Beirut, he meant to attack on his way home, for to leave these cities in possession of the Christians would be the greatest help in case of another crusade.

The king had arranged for the two queens and their ladies, who had been staying at Acre, to return on the same ship in which they had come; and having made all his plans, he was in his tent, only waiting for morning to sail off in his royal galley, the *Trenchmer*, whose crimson sails and hull gleamed in the moonlight as it rode at anchor in the Bay of Acre. The two pages had not yet parted, as Count William was going on one of the ships that were to sail with the *Trenchmer*, so the boys expected to bed together again at Beriut.

As Richard sat now within his tent, playing softly on his lute, while Hugh was busy gathering up the last of his baggage, suddenly they heard the sound of horses galloping on the hard sand of the shore. Nearer and nearer they came, till the riders drew rein in front of the royal tent and sprang to the ground as Hugh ran to let them in.

They were two messengers, breathless and spent from the haste of their long ride. Kneeling at his feet and saluting the king. "Sire," burst out one of them, "thank God you are still here! We feared we might be too late! We come straight from Jaffa to implore help, for the city is sore beset! Saladin's army, a mighty host, surrounds it, and though the garrison you left and the townspeople have defended themselves so bravely that they have drawn praise even from the enemy, they have been driven to the citadel as a last refuge. The sultan has given them five days of grace, and if no succor comes, everyman, woman and child must first pay a heavy tribute of gold, and then surrender themselves and all the sick and wounded there to the mercy of the infidels."

"Living Lord!" broke in King Richard before the messenger could say more, "God willing, I will do what I can!" He thought a moment, then, "Hugh!" he called. "Quick,lad!" and he dispatched the page instantly to the tents of Count William and seven other chosen knights still in the camp, and sent a squire to go swiftly to the palaces in Acre where lived the Masters of the Knights of the Temple and of St. John. These were all to come at once to the royal tent, where they soon arrived and by midnight had made their plans. Richard, with eight knights and their men, were to sail down the coast to Jaffa, as this was the quickest way to get there. The Knights of the Temple and of St. John were to gather together, besides their own companies, as many as possible of the Christians who lived in Palestine, and march as fast as they could to help the king.

Neither Hugh nor Raymond slept much the rest of the night; their heads were too full of excitement. As it had been expected the galleys would leave early in the morning anyway, with but little more preparation they were ready, and by noon off they sailed, Count William and his men on the *Trenchmer* with King Richard, and the other knights and their followers filling a few more ships. They were at best only a little handful to face the great army of Saladin, but the Lion Heart was dauntless and his brave followers took fresh courage from him.

As the crimson sails of the galley puffed and filled, the two pages leaned over the rail, watching the coast with its palms and olives and the square flat-roofed houses of the towns and villiages they passed as they sped along. The summer sun beat scorchingly on the sandy shore, and "My!" said Raymond, "aren't you glad we are going back to Jaffa by water instead of marching along that blistering road, looking out for scorpions and spiders and thorns all the while?"

"Yes, indeed!" replied Hugh. "This is really fine, and we're going pretty fast. If the wind holds out, it won't take us long to get there." But scarcely were the words out of his mouth when suddenly the wind failed; the bright sails flapped and hung motionless, and soon the galley lay becalmed, and of course the other ships were in the same plight. For nearly three days they could make no headway. Everyone was in despair, and King Richard paced up and down the deck of the *Trenchmer* like a caged lion.

But at last, late on the third day, "Pull! Puff!" the wind sprang up again. Again the sails swelled and fluttered as they hurried southward. Two more days the ships skimmed over the waves; and then, "This is the fifth day!" whispered Hugh to Raymond as they hung over the water. "If we don't get to Jaffa tonight it will be too late!" But they did! At midnight the captain of the galley told the king they were entering the harbor of Jaffa; but Richard bade him cast anchor till morning, as before landing he must find out whether the garrison in the citadel still held out or had been forced to surrender that evening.

At the first streak of dawn everyone on the ships was straining his eyes toward land, and what they saw was enough to daunt the bravest, but not the bold hearts of the crusaders. The shore was covered with tents from which poured an innumerable host of Saracens, brandishing their weapons, beating their brazen drums, and, as usual, yelling at the tops of their voices.

As King Richard looked toward the citadel, which joined the Jaffa walls inside, trying to think quickly of some way of getting the news he wanted, suddenly, *"Look! Look!"* cried Hugh, pointing breathlessly to its battlements. A man was seen standing there, and in another moment making his way to the top of the city wall, he leaped down. A hillock of sand beneath it saved him from hurt, and springing to his feet, amid a shower of arrows from the Saracens he plunged into the sea, swimming with all his might and main toward the *Trenchmer;* for the red sails of the royal galley had been seen far off by the watchers in the citadel, and they knew the king would want to know whether they had yet surrendered.

Richard was the first to receive the bold swimmer as wet and panting he clambered up the side of the ship, and the moment he heard the garrison still helf out, though it was the very morning fixed for its surrender, turning to the captain who awaited his orders, "Steer straight for shore!" he commanded. As the red keel flew toward the land, again came a volley of arrows from the enemy, but the instant the galley reached shallower water, and before the anchor could be cast, hanging his shield around his neck and leaping into the sea, the Lion Heart rushed to shore, waving his great battle-ax before him, and followed at once by Count William and the other knights.

All the Christians fought with the greatest bravery, but

Richard was like a very demon. Always reckless of danger, and now more reckless than ever, perhaps because of his disappointment in the crusade, he hewed to right and left, cleaving for himself a broad path of killed and wounded. At first the Saracens tried to fight back, but in an amazingly short while they were seized with a panic. The terror of his name and the terrific blows he was dealing struck fear to their hearts, till wildly shrieking,

"The Malek Ric! The Malek Ric!" all that great host of them took to their heels and fled in every direction. Some rushed into the city, pursued by Richard, who joined by the garrison there, drove them from street to street till few were left alive; when he went outside again with his little handful of men to face those of the flying Saracens whom Saladin had managed to rally together, the moment they saw him, once more terror seized them. All, even the sultan himself, fled again, leaving their entire camp in the hands of the crusaders.

The two pages, who had watched the fight from the deck of the *Trenchmer*, too absorbed to say a word, now hurried excitedly to land, shouting with delight at the fiery dash and fury with which the king and his little band had won the day; and they soon were busy helping in their masters' tents as they were pitched for camping. For all was not yet over at Jaffa. Saladin, though beaten that morning, had not given up hope of taking the city; and Richard, guessing this, decided not to leave at once, but to wait and see. Besides, he was expecting the little troop which was marching down the coast; this arrived in a couple of days, and though all were much disappointed to have come too late for the fight on the shore, they need not have worried, for there was plenty more in store for them.

Meantime the sultan, who was still planning to attack Jaffa again, had heard that Count Henry of Champagne had got together some more soldiers from around Tyre and was coming to help Richard; so, leaving a small force to watch Jaffa, he hurried off to try to prevent the count from getting there. Then, as king and sultan managed to keep pretty good track of each other's moves in this game of war, Richard at once sent off as many men as he could possibly spare to help Count Henry. When Saladin found that out, he changed his mind about fighting the count, and began to rush his big army back as fast as he could to try to crush Richard's little army while it was the very smallest.—There! Can you keep all that straight in your head?—And it was all very quickly done; for as the sultan was hurrying back to Jaffa, evening had fallen on only the third day after the battle on the shore.

Richard was in his tent, which he had recklessly caused to be pitched in the camp outside the city walls, instead of within them as everybody thought he ought to. He was tired, and presently he called Hugh to bring him water and comb his hair, which always seemed to soothe him, and before long he was sleeping soundly, and a little later Hugh himself lay in his narrow bed in a small part curtained from the main tent.

The little new moon rose and set; and the page, though a

light sleeper, did not waken till in the dusk just before dawn, when suddenly with a startled feeling his eyes flew open. Bewildered and but half awake, he lay still for a moment, when he caught the murmur of whispered voices outside the tent; for, as it was very hot, this was but loosely fastened. At the same instant, as he was trying to listen to these, his eyes, grown used to the darkness, could make out the stooping figure of a man within the tent who seemed to be crawling on his hands and knees toward that part where the king slept.

Hugh, now wide awake and alert, lost not another moment. Jumping from his bed, he sprang clear over the man, and in one stride was at his master's side, shouting, *"Wake up! Wake up, Sire!"*

Richard sat up, dazed at first, and then a streak of dawn lighting the darkness, the man quickly straightened up, and evidently determined to risk all, rushed at him and tried to plunge a dagger into his heart. But the instant he came near, the king, with a steely gleam in his eyes, reached out one hand, and seizing him by the throat, held him like a vise till the knights and squires close by, who had been roused by Hugh's shouts, came hurrying in, when with a contemptuous shake he flung him to them to be dealt with later as he deserved. Then turning to Hugh, "Lad," said the king, taking Hugh's hand between his own, "you have saved my life, it seems. Had not you wakened me, yonder coward would have stabbed me while I slept. I shall not forget what you have done, my boy."

RICHARD SAT UP, DAZED AT FIRST.

Hugh flushed with pleasure as the others crowded about to hear what had happened. Then getting together a band of soldiers, the knights hurried out to scour the surrounding hills for the man's companions, though they did not find them. They were part of the force left by Saladin to watch Jaffa, and had decided to try to capture or kill King Richard while asleep in his tent. But when they came there, their boldness left them, and they had disputed so long as to who should creep in that the dawn had almost overtaken them; and those outside the tent, when they heard Hugh's shout, had leaped on their horses and ridden off like the wind. It is but fair to say, though, that what they had planned was no doubt entirely their own idea and that Saladin himself knew nothing at all about it; for he would have been far too chivalrous to attempt the life of his royal foe in so cowardly a way.

But since luckily, Richard escaped harm, it was just as well that the crusaders were roused early, for they had a hard day's work ahead of them. As the summer sun rose higher, it was not long before they began to see in the distance the vanguard of Saladin's army, which you know was hurrying down to try to crush the English king. When Richard saw the great hosts of turbaned Saracens coming closer, he quickly gathered together his own little force, standing with their backs to the sea, and told them no man must flinch for a single instant; for while, if defeated, the Saracens could easily retreat to the hills, for the crusaders the coming battle meant victory or death, since, if beaten, they would be driven into the sea. Hugh and Raymond, who had crowded near, felt their hearts leap as they listened to his words; they were wild to be in the fight, but were obliged as usual to obey orders and keep to one side when it began.

And it began soon enough. As the Saracens came galloping down, the crusader knights sprang on their horses, Richard on Favelle ahead of all, and rushed to meet them; and from that moment the wild battle was on. When it had lasted about an hour, the two pages, who were anxious to see it and could not well do so from the low shore where they stood, decided to try to get inside the city and climb up on its wall so they could look down on the sandy plain where the fight was going on. This they managed to do, and watched eagerly as the battle surged to and fro. It was a thrilling scene; but towering above the struggling mass of men, the Lion Heart, always in the thickest of the fight, charging furiously to right and left, often entirely surrounded by the enemy but always gallantly cleaving his way through, rescuing those of his knights who were unhorsed, smiting down the boldest of the infidels, and performing unheard-of deeds of bravery, it was his figure that held the boy's eyes above all others.

"He seems everywhere at once!" cried Hugh. "And his battle-ax flashes like a streak of lightning!"

Just then, *"Oh!"* exclaimed Raymond. *"Look! An arrow has hit Favelle!"*

Sure enough, pierced by a Saracen dart, the brave warhorse was dying; but as he sank to the ground, Richard, quickly freeing himself from the stirrups, sprang to his feet and struck out with his battle-ax, felling all who came near him.

"There, see!" cried Hugh despairingly, "The Saracens are closing around him! I don't see how even he can hold out!"

But he did, keeping a circle cleared around him. "I wonder why some of our knights don't get him another horse?" said Raymond.

"He's so far in the enemy's lines I suppose they don't see him," replied Hugh, "and besides they are so busy fighting themselves,—but"—here both boys stared in amazement,— *"will you look at that!"*

They could make out a Nubian slave waving above his head a white flag of truce and swiftly forcing his way among the struggling men toward King Richard. He was followed by two others leading a pair of the finest Arabian horses, saddled and bridled, their silky coats shining as they stepped prancingly along. Pausing in front of Richard and bowing low, they seemed to be presenting them to him; for, quickly choosing, he sprang on the back of one, and in another moment was again in the thick of the fight, while the slaves led the other horse through the crusader lines and gave him in charge of a squire to keep ready in case the king needed another.

The pages drew a long breath. "Do—do you suppose *Saladin* sent those?" said Raymond, bewildered.

"It looks like it!" replied Hugh, "Let's go find out!" And they both hurried down and ran to where the beautiful Arab charger was arching his neck and pawing the ground. And sure enough, as the boys had guessed, the horses had been sent, in the true spirit of chivalry, from Richard's Saracen foes. It seems the sultan and his brother, Malek Adel, were not in the battle themselves, as was the English king, but watching and directing it from a little hillock near by. When Favelle fell to the ground someone pointed out Richard to Saladin. "What!" cried the sultan, "the English king fighting on foot like a common soldier? That is not right!" and turning to his attendants, he at once ordered two of his choicest horses to be taken instantly to Richard with the compliments of himself and Malek Adel. And the Lion Heart, most chivalrous of kings, had accepted them in the same spirit in which they were sent.

Meantime the battle was going on furiously; arrows flying, lances and spears, battle-axes, swords and scimitars all dealing deadly blows; yet still the brave little band of crusaders stood their ground, and of the heaps of slain that strewed the sands by far the greater number were Saracens.

Toward noon there was a lull in the fighting, both sides feeling the need of rest and food; so the two armies drew apart for awhile, facing each other with a narrow space between. Presently a murmur of surprise ran along the lines and our two pages, crowding up as near as they could, saw King Richard riding slowly along in front of the Saracens; he was waving his battle-ax and daring any champion among them to come out and fight him. On he rode, down the whole long line of turbaned enemies, but not one of them stirred from the ranks. There were many brave warriors among them, but all drew back at the thought of fighting single-handed with "The Malek Ric."

Hugh's eyes glowed with pride in his master as the latter, with a contemptuous shrug, rode slowly back to the middle of the space dividing the armies. And then both pages stared again, for what do you suppose he did? Deliberately getting off his horse, he sat down and called for something to eat! When the word was passed along, some of Richard's squires hurried to the army cooks, and one of them was coming bearing a tray, when Hugh, seeing him, sprang out and demanded it. "It's my right to carry food to the king and wait on him while he eats!" he exclaimed.

"What, boy?" said the squire in surprise, "But you're not old enough to be a soldier, and those infidels yonder may let their arrows fly any minute. Though they are afraid to fight him singly, "The Malek Ric" is a pretty tempting mark as he sits boldly there on the ground!"

"Well," said Hugh, drawing himself up very straight, "I guess I am no coward, if I am only a page! It's your right to cut his meat for him, but I'm going to take it to him!" And seizing the tray, he hurried off as fast as he could toward his royal master, a couple of squires following to do the carving.

As panting and breathless Hugh set the tray down in front of King Richard, the latter smiled his approval. "You are a brave lad," he said, "and will make a good knight when you win your spurs." Hugh looked his delight as he stood by the king's side ready to give him any service. And he soon saw something to do. "Shall I pull some of the arrows from your armor, Sire?" he ventured to ask. "I think they will be in your way while you eat."

"Why, yes," said Richard, carelessly looking down at his hauberk bristling with arrows whose tips had stuck in the steel rings they could not pierce through, "I am as full of Saracen darts as a hedgehog of spines. But be quick about it! We have not much time to lose!"

Hugh tugged and pulled and got out the arrows that were most in the way; and then the moment the king had finished eating, off he flew with the tray, and quickly returning with a ewer and basin, poured water over his master's hands, drying them as usual on a napkin he had brought. When this was done, "Now scamper off lad!" said Richard as, rising to his feet, he sprang on his horse.

The Saracens, who while "The Malek Ric" had been eating, had looked on in silent astonishment, now took this as a signal to renew the battle; and through all the long hot afternoon it raged unceasingly. Again and again the forces of Saladin swept down upon them in furious charges, but nothing could daunt the courage of the crusaders who fought with their backs to the sea. At last, toward evening, baffled and discouraged, the fierce shouts of the Saracens died away, their brazen drums sounded a retreat, and they fled to the hills, leaving hundreds of their bravest warriors dead upon the field.

The final battle of Jaffa was over and the crusaders were the victors. It had been won by sheer bravery, a small band fighting against enormous odds. Of Richard's part in it, those who knew him best declared that for deeds of heroic daring and boldness no one had ever equaled him. The battle of Assur had been a fierce and courageous struggle, but the battle of Jaffa was longer and harder fought and the victory more amazing; and it was Richard's bravery and heroism that all day long kept up the courage of the rest. Indeed, it is no wonder that the name of the Lion Heart struck such terror to the Saracens that for years and years—perhaps they do so yet, for all I know—they made of him a bogie to frighten their children into obedience. If their little ones were naughty, "Come," they would say, "you had better mind quickly, or *The Malek Ric* will catch you!"

CHAPTER XII

The Return Home

The Sultan was so mortified over his defeat at Jaffa that he shut himself up in his tent for three days and would see no one. When he recovered enough to talk to people again, Richard proposed a truce. He had tried to make a truce before, for he hated to go back to his kingdom unless he could leave the Christians in the Holy Land at peace, at least until he could start another crusade and come back again.

But Saladin had been unwilling to agree to Richard's terms. Now, however, subdued by the battle of Jaffa, he finally made the truce. For three years, three months, three weeks and three days (and three hours, three minutes and three seconds? Very likely, though history writers have forgotten to mention it) the Saracens were to let the cities alone which the crusaders had taken and where the garrisons were to stay, and pilgrims were to visit Jerusalem and the Holy Sepulchre without being molested. There were many other terms to the truce, but never mind them here.

When at last all was arranged, Richard was once more ready to start for home, which he was anxious to reach as soon as possible, for the news from there was all the while worse and worse. He gave up his plan of attacking Beirut on the way, and also changed his mind about sailing on the *Trenchmer* with the little fleet of ships, for his enemies could then keep track of his movements and perhaps lay traps for him. He decided instead to go back by land and in disguise, so he could reach home quietly and then make his plans as seemed best. Of course Hugh went with Him? No; to the great sorrow of the boy and the regret of Richard himself, he could not take him. Why not? Well, that was because, as he was going disguised and did not wish more than one page attending him, the thought it better to take a boy who could speak German, as he would have to pass through Austria and Germany and did not know their language himself. Now one of the knights who had not yet sailed away happened to have such a page, so it was he who went with the king; the latter, however, when he parted from Hugh, praised him warmly for the faithful service he had given, and especially for that night in the tent when the lad's watchfulness had saved his life. Then he gave him a wonderful jewel for his cap and a beautiful clasp for his cloak, and told him that when he returned to England he hoped, if possible, to take him again into his service.

Alas, Richard little guessed how long it would be before he reached his kingdom again! I have not time here to tell you of his thrilling adventures on the way home; of how, while passing through Austria, he was made prisoner by the spiteful Duke Leopold, who for two whole years kept him captive in a castle dungeon; nor of his romantic release through the singing of a song. But by and by you will read all this elsewhere, and

HE GAVE HIM A WONDERFUL JEWEL FOR HIS CAP.

when you have begun the story, I am sure you will find it so fascinating you will not stop till you have finished.

As for the two pages, after a safe voyage to the city of Marseilles, on the southern coast of France, they were obliged to part, though with many heartaches, for they cared greatly for each other. Raymond returned with Count William, and Hugh went with a company of English knights through King Richard's French possessions and thence to England; and both lads took up the life they had left more than a year before. When they were old enough, Raymond received knighthood at the hands of his master; while to Hugh's great joy, it was his good fortune to kneel before King Richard, who striking his shoulder lightly with his sword, pronounced the words, 'In the name of God and St. Michael and St.George I dub thee knight!' Hugh's own sword, a fine Damascus blade with beautiful jeweled hilt and scabbard inlaid with gold and silver, was a gift from the king, as were also his handsome spurs. But the newmade knight was destined never again to follow his master to the Holy Land, as he had hoped. In the seven years since his return to England Richard had found such difficult affairs of his own to attend to that he had been unable to start another crusade as he had wished, and his death in France a year later forever put an end to his dreams.

What good did the crusades do? Well, that is a rather hard question to answer. You know I told you there were seven in all, the one of our story being the third; yet, though none after the first succeeded in conquering Jerusalem, they did much for the world in other ways. The people of Europe and of Asia came to know each other better, and each learned many, many things from the other. And while it may seem strange to us that for hundreds of years so many men should flock so far, fight so bitterly and suffer so much for the sake of an empty tomb, even though the tomb of our Saviour, nevertheless, to them it was an ideal full of holiness and reverence. And no one can fight for a high ideal and be willing to lay down his life for it without being the better because of it. It is perhaps true that many took the cross more from a wish to win fame as soldiers than to save the Sepulchre; indeed, it is said by some that Richard himself did so. But we must remember that at the time of the crusades people cared much more for fighting for its own sake than we do today; and after all, it was but natural that the brave knights, and common soldiers, too, should want to gain glory, and no one has a right to say that they ever forgot the sacred cause for which they had come.

Hugh and Raymond, I am sure never forgot their year in Palestine though they served there only as pages. And if they met in after-life, as I dare say they did, they must have talked it over many times; and I am sure, too, that the memory of much they had seen there must have been an inspiration to them as long as they lived. For with all their quarrels and failures, the men of the third crusade and their lion-hearted leader left a lasting record of gallant and heroic deeds.